SPARTAN WARRIOR

BIRTH ΩF A
WARRIΩR

SPARTAN WARRIOR

BIRTH OF A WARRIOR

MICHAEL FORD

BLOOMSBURY

First published in Great Britain in 2008 by
Bloomsbury Publishing Plc
36 Soho Square, London, W1D 3QY

986,570/ SF

A CIP catalogue record of this book is available from the
British Library

ISBN 978 0 7475 9387 4

Typeset by Dorchester Typesetting Group Ltd
Printed in Great Britain by Clays Ltd, St Ives Plc

1 3 5 7 9 10 8 6 4 2

www.bloomsbury.com

For Rebecca

PROLOGUE

Lysander circled his opponent. Each breath scorched his lungs and he could feel his arms being dragged down by the weight of his armour. He blinked away the sweat that stung his eyes.

Demaratos stared back at him, his eyes filled with hate. Lysander swung an arm at his opponent, but Demaratos skipped out of the way and smirked. The spectators let out a raucous cheer.

He's too strong, *thought Lysander.*

Lysander scanned the crowd again, looking for his grandfather, Sarpedon. He wasn't there.

Demaratos lunged forward. His fist caught Lysander in the gut and he collapsed to his knees, trying to suck in air. None came. Lysander felt as though he were drowning. Demaratos punched him again, this time in the face. There was no pain, but he toppled sideways, crashing into the sand. He couldn't move.

It was over.

Demaratos lifted his hands in the air and the crowd roared. A figure came forward to offer him the prize. It was

Lysander's cousin, Kassandra. She held a wreath of olive leaves over Demaratos's head. But as she lowered the wreath, it transformed into a leather thong with a red pendant. The Fire of Ares.

'That's mine!' cried Lysander, but no one listened. No one cared.

The scene changed. Lysander found himself beside a cart that carried a linen-shrouded body. His mother. The grave was to one side of the path, a black hole in the earth. Lysander turned back to the cart, and saw that Orpheus and Leonidas had appeared beside the body. They were here to bury his mother.

Orpheus took the head and Leonidas the feet. Lysander wanted to help, but he stood rooted to the spot, unable to move.

Then the shrouded body twitched.

'Wait!' shouted Lysander. He tried to stop them from lowering his mother into the grave, but his feet were like ice-cold marble.

The legs of the body were twisting now.

'She's alive,' shouted Lysander. 'Can't you see? She's not dead!'

But Orpheus and Leonidas paid no attention. They carried the writhing body to the edge of the grave. Lysander could feel an iciness climbing up through his chest, where his heart thumped with fear. There wasn't long left. Orpheus moved to one edge of the grave and Leonidas to the other. The body of his mother, struggling weakly in their grasp, hung above the black hole in the ground.

'Please!' Lysander begged. 'Don't drop her! She's alive. Please, you're my friends!'

Neither Orpheus nor Leonidas looked up. Lysander's mother disappeared into the blackness.

CHAPTER 1

'No!' Lysander shouted. He sat bolt upright in bed, his chest heaving with panic.

'Shut your mouth, half-breed!' hissed Demaratos from the other side of the room. Straining his eyes against the gloom, Lysander could make out the shapes of his fellow students huddled beneath their cloaks. They lay in rows on their mattresses of river rushes, one along either wall of the narrow, low-beamed dormitory.

'Another nightmare?' mumbled Orpheus sleepily from the bed beside him.

'Yes,' whispered Lysander.

'Quiet!' ordered Demaratos. 'Or I'll give you something to have a nightmare about.'

Lysander lay back on his bed of rushes, waiting for the terror of the dream to seep from his veins.

Wind buffeted the barracks, howling along the walls. Summer was long gone and chill air fell heavily from the mountains. The timbers creaked ominously and somewhere a hatch banged. Lysander pulled his cloak more tightly around his shoulders and brought his hand up to rest on the pendant that hung from his neck. The Fire of Ares.

Lysander turned over in his bed, trying to get comfortable. Since the early summer, his life had been transformed. Without the family pendant – the red stone mounted in bronze – Lysander would never have learnt the truth. He would not have discovered that his grandfather, Sarpedon, was one of the most powerful men in Sparta; that his father was not a Helot of the fields, but a Spartan warrior, killed before he was even born. For thirteen years his life had been a lie. But his mother had shared the truth with him in the end.

His new existence wasn't without danger. Lysander would forever be known as the half-breed 'mothax' who had stood in the way of rebellion and humiliated the Spartans. He had saved his grandfather from the hands of murderous Helots. Lysander had been victorious at the annual Festival Games. But at what cost? His nightmare told him how easily his victory could have turned to defeat.

Burying his head into his cloak, Lysander recalled the second part of his nightmare, a twisted version of his mother's funeral. Two days after his victory at the Games, accompanied by his grandfather Sarpedon and his cousin Kassandra, he had made his way to the family tomb on the southern road out of the city. Orpheus and Leonidas hadn't been there. Nor had there been any party of hired mourners wailing their dirges to the Gods. The death of a Helot woman didn't merit it. Instead, his mother's body had ridden on a cart pulled by a single mule.

At the grave site, beside the low marble stone that marked his father's resting place, the Helots from his mother's settlement had lowered Athenasia into the ground. Lysander had placed her few possessions on top of the linen: an ivory comb, and a bracelet hung with small iridescent shells.

Now, he felt hot tears on his cheeks and he dug his face further into his cloak, trying to mask his sobs from the rest of the barracks.

'I miss you,' Lysander whispered into the night. Then he closed his eyes and tried to sleep again, praying that the nightmares would stay away.

Suddenly the quiet dormitory was filled with the sound of pounding feet. Lysander's bed was surrounded by dark shadows – tall black shapes against the wall. One was shorter than the others and stood back a little. Lysander scrambled up the bed and pulled his cloak protectively around his shoulders.

'What's happening?' he asked, trying to make out faces in the darkness. Strong hands gripped his ankles and hauled him across the floor. Lysander reached out, trying to find something to grab on to. His attackers dragged him by his feet towards the door, the muscles of his back catching on the packed earth. The other students were awake now, craning round in their beds to see what the commotion was about.

'What's all the noise?' said a sleepy voice.

But only one student left his bed to help – Lysander's friend, Orpheus. He clambered to his feet and came forward, leaning on his stick.

'Leave him alone!' he said.

One of the men pushed him roughly to the floor. 'Crawl back into your bed, cripple!' he spat.

Lysander managed to kick free and scrambled to his knees.

'Don't touch him!' He threw himself at the soldier, but a foot slammed into his back and the men closed round him again. A hand grabbed the back of his neck, and a coarse hemp sack was pulled over his head. A cord tied the hood down, biting into his flesh.

Complete darkness. The damp smell of the hemp filled his nostrils and he could feel his breathing become quick and shallow as panic flooded him. *What are they going to do to me?* he thought.

Someone punched him in the side of the head and Lysander fell sideways. He collided with another body and that person shouldered him off. Lysander lost his bearings and tripped into something hard – a wall or doorway.

'He can't even walk straight,' mocked a man's voice.

A final shove sent Lysander out into the cold night air. He stumbled over what must have been the threshold and he fell on to the ground, crying out in pain. He couldn't put his hands out to break his fall and his head cracked against a rock. Blood trickled down his temple.

'What do you want?' he said, his hot breath muffled inside the hood.

'Keep your mouth shut, half-breed!' someone said gruffly.

More than one man took hold of his arms and waist and he was hoisted into the air. His hands touched something warm. Coarse short fur bristled beneath his fingers and an animal smell filled his nostrils. A horse. His legs were tugged into position either side of the beast's back. Feeling the live, twitching animal beneath him brought a cold feeling of dread. Someone mounted in front of him. Unbalanced, Lysander gripped the other rider's waist. There was a grunt and the horse moved forward.

As they rode, Lysander buried his head against the back of his kidnapper. His mind reeled. Where were they taking him?

He wasn't sure how long they rode for, but as the horse juddered to a halt, Lysander's mind suddenly cleared. If he was going to be killed now, he would meet his death bravely. Hands pulled him off the back of the horse and he thumped to the ground on his side. His breath escaped him and panic filled his chest. He tried to suck in some air. The cord was untied and the hood whipped away.

He could see little at first: the stony ground, a few bushes and the dark silhouettes of cloaked figures. A blow to his ear dizzied him, and he sank to the ground.

'Hold him down!'

The voice was distant. Nothing happened.

'I said, hold him down!'

The sole of a sandal pressed his face into the dirt. The earth tasted damp and gritty against his lips. Lysander didn't struggle. He was defenceless. At any moment the blade of a sword would end his life.

It didn't come.

His eyes had time to adjust to the faint moonlight. At the edges of his vision, Lysander saw thick swathes of cloud sweeping through the blue-black sky. The person pinning Lysander down shifted his weight, relieving the pressure on Lysander's head. He turned his neck and managed to glimpse the face of his attacker. For a moment the dizziness returned.

This didn't make any sense.

The figure standing above him looked back. His sandy hair was messy, as though he too had been woken from his bed. He stared at Lysander, his eyes wide with fear. Then the boy shot a glance back at the other men.

'Sorry,' he said, unable to look back down at Lysander.

It was Timeon.

CHAPTER 2

Timeon was Lysander's friend. The boy who had come to the barracks to serve as his slave. They'd known each other for as long as Lysander could remember.

'Why?'

Timeon didn't answer. Something wasn't right. A red graze scored his cheekbone.

'I didn't want to . . .' he began, his lip trembling, but he was yanked away. Lysander could see some of his attackers more clearly now. The moonlight reflected in their eyes as they stared at him. Their features were set stern like granite. The black cloaks told Lysander exactly who they were. The Krypteia. The Hidden Ones. The Spartan death squads who terrorised the lives of innocent Helots and killed without mercy.

Another familiar face came into view. Diokles. Since the night of the Festival Games, the barracks tutor had given Lysander a wide berth, but he had always suspected that revenge would come. There was no way Diokles would forget the humiliation of being at the mercy of a Helot – he was missing several teeth where a thresher had caught him across the jaw. Diokles crouched beside Lysander and cocked his head to one side. Lysander struggled to hold his gaze as the tutor leant forward. Lysander knew that Diokles was one of the Krypteia.

'What's happening?' asked Lysander. He was ashamed at how weak and small his voice sounded. The look in his tutor's good eye was as cold as the wind. Diokles sneered.

'Surely, Lysander, son of Thorakis, you will not suffer such offence?' He pointed to where Timeon was standing. 'A Helot's foot grinding your face into the dirt?'

'They made me do –' Timeon blurted out. A hand grabbed him by the throat and dragged him backwards, choking his words out of him.

'A slave's foot in the face of a Spartan warrior-in-training?' Diokles went on. 'It cannot be tolerated.'

Timeon's face was turning red as the Spartan continued to squeeze his throat.

'Don't hurt him,' pleaded Lysander.

Diokles chuckled.

'Oh, *I* won't hurt him, boy. But *you* will.'

Lysander swallowed back the dread that rose in his throat.

'What do you mean?' he asked.

Diokles pushed his thumb hard against the gash on Lysander's head. Lysander gritted his teeth, determi not to show his pain. Diokles pulled back his hand – the pad of his thumb was smeared in Lysander's blood.

'The offence was given to you,' said his tutor. 'So you must repay it.' Understanding washed over Lysander. Diokles' one good eye glinted coldly. 'Blood, for blood.'

'No,' said Timeon. 'Please, Lysander, they came to my home, they threatened my family. My mother, my sister Sophia. I had to do what they told me . . .'

Timeon was thrown to the ground. One of the black-cloaked Spartans kicked him hard in the stomach, forcing Timeon to curl up into a ball. Diokles drew himself up to his full height and spoke more loudly now, addressing Lysander so the rest of the men could hear.

'A Helot enters a Spartan barracks at night. He drags a Spartan from his bed and humiliates him in front of his peers. I ask you again, Lysander, what will you do about this insult?'

Lysander climbed painfully to his feet and looked at Timeon, who was still sitting hunched on the ground. The five members of the Krypteia stood around, like black crows eyeing carrion in the fields. Lysander didn't know what was expected of him. He sensed any answer would be the wrong one.

'I won't do anything,' said Lysander quietly. 'I shall be lenient.'

Diokles barked with laughter. 'That's ridiculous! At the very least he must be flogged until his blood soaks the earth.'

'No, please . . .' whimpered Timeon.

Diokles gave a curt nod to his comrades. One of them seized Timeon by the elbow and hauled him to his feet. He was pushed forward and jostled up a nearby slope. Diokles seized Lysander and dragged him in the same direction. Suddenly Lysander realised where they were – it was the bottom end of the Helot settlement, near where he and his mother used to live. As they came over the crown of the hillock, the low huts of the Helot village came into sight, and the air filled with the sounds of wailing and moans.

Torches lit the way along the tracks between the houses, and Spartan soldiers were standing guard outside the huts.

From the doorway of one, Lysander saw an elderly man fall to the ground, then crawl forward on his hands and knees. Lysander recognised him as Hector, Timeon's uncle. A Spartan soldier stepped up to him and delivered a blow to his back with the flat side of his sword.

'Hurry! I don't have all night.' An elderly woman stumbled out of the same house. As the moonlight caught her face, Lysander recognised Melantho, Timeon's aunt.

'Please, don't hurt him,' she pleaded. 'He's a harmless farmer.' Another soldier pushed her to the ground.

All along the pathways between the houses, Helot men were being dragged from their houses and into the streets. The women – mothers, sisters and daughters

– rushed about, screaming and crying, and were pushed away.

Timeon was forced towards a water trough. A horizontal wooden bar at waist level lined the rim of the trough. Diokles shoved Lysander in the back.

'Put your hands on the post,' said one of the Spartans. Timeon looked at Lysander, fear crumpling his face as tears streamed down his cheeks. How had it come to this? Half a year before they were boys working in the fields, looking after each other. Now his best friend was being terrorised and there was nothing Lysander could do.

The man beside Timeon thrust an open-handed blow into his midriff and Timeon doubled over, steadying himself with his hands on the wooden bar, and choking for breath. Two of the Krypteia bound his hands to the post.

'Prepare the others!' shouted Diokles. As the order was passed down the streets, Lysander saw men being tied to doorposts or lintels. The Spartans standing over Hector pulled him by his arms, his thin knees dragging in the dirt. Timeon's uncle was lashed to the rim of an upright barrel. The soldiers were readying canes and whips. Revenge was being taken at last. This was payback for the rebellion of two months before. The truth hit Lysander like one of Zeus's thunderbolts: this was all his doing. He had been the one who persuaded the Helots to go back to their homes that night. He had told them they would not be harmed. *No, wait*, he thought, *my grandfather guaranteed their safety as well. He wouldn't let this happen.*

'You have to stop this,' he said to Diokles. 'Sarpedon promised the Helots that there would be no retribution for their uprising.'

'The old Ephor said what he needed to so that his throat would not be cut,' shot back Diokles. The tutor took a polished horn from his belt, and brought it to his lips. He looked at Lysander. 'Helots don't dictate the rules to Spartans. We command them, and now it's time to show them that we are still their masters.' He blew a signal. A Spartan brought his rod down across Hector's back. He wailed as he fell to his knees. Another crack sounded further down the street. Moans of pain and cries of anguish swelled to fill the night air. Lysander didn't need to see each blow to realise what was happening. The whole settlement was being punished.

One of the Krypteia held out a whip to Lysander.

'Take it!' ordered Diokles.

Lysander looked at the instrument of punishment.

Timeon was shivering with fear now, his eyes shifting from Diokles to Lysander. Diokles snatched the whip and thrust it into Lysander's hand.

The tightly-bound leather weighed heavy in his hand. Lysander knew all too well the damage it could do. He was no stranger to the bite of a whip against his own back. There were knots tied along the length of the leather, designed to tear open skin.

'He's my friend. I can't do it.'

Diokles seized the back of Lysander's neck and pushed his face towards the water trough. He spat into the water beside Lysander.

'Your friend? He's a Helot. You're a Spartan. He's not your friend. He's your property.' Timeon's face was reflected in the still water. 'I knew you were trouble from the start. Let's see what your precious pendant can do for you now, shall we?'

Lysander was trapped. For a moment his eyes caught Timeon's glance in the trough water. What could he do?

Timeon gazed at Lysander. Then he gave a small nod.

He's giving me permission, thought Lysander. It felt as though his heart would break. He couldn't believe that his friend had to go through this humiliation in order to save Lysander. Anger surged through him and he threw down the whip at Diokles' feet.

'I won't do it!' he shouted. 'Punish me, instead.'

The tutor's eye widened, but then he grinned. He stooped and picked up the whip. He nodded in the direction of the huts, where Lysander could still hear the regular crack of whips and the groans of pain. Diokles' eye narrowed to a slit.

'That won't end until you do your duty as a Spartan.'

His duty. So this was it.

'Whip Timeon and it will stop,' said Diokles in his ear.

So I can end this, thought Lysander, *but at what cost?*

'Do it!' shouted Timeon. 'Just do it.'

16

With a trembling hand, Lysander took the handle of the whip from Diokles. He pulled back his arm, letting the leather uncoil to the ground.

'May the Gods forgive me,' he whispered. With a flick of his wrist, he brought the lash down across Timeon's back.

His friend let out a cry of agony, and Lysander saw his knuckles tighten on the post.

'It gets easier after the first,' shouted one of the Spartans, and the others laughed.

His friend gave another nod. Lysander swung the whip again. And again. Timeon writhed with every blow. On the fifth stroke, something wet splattered across Lysander's face. It was his friend's blood. Timeon moaned, but his eyes met Lysander's once again. Pain had forced a glistening sheen of sweat to his skin. Lysander lost count of the strokes. His own muscles burned as he drew back his arm time after time. Finally he heard Diokles blow the horn once again. The sounds of the flogging were replaced by that of weeping. Lysander's own face was wet with tears. One of the Krypteia drew his dagger and cut Timeon's bonds. His friend slumped to the earth.

A small group of women emerged from between the huts of the settlement.

'Timeon?' said a female voice unsurely. One girl had broken away from the group. It was Sophia, Timeon's younger sister. 'Brother! Timeon!' she cried as she fell to her knees, throwing her arms around him. Timeon groaned softly, his eyes only half open. Sophia looked down at her hands, now covered in blood. Her look of grief vanished when she caught sight of Lysander. Her face registered puzzlement, then horror. Lysander was speechless and light-headed. How could this be happening? How could he explain?

Diokles took the whip from Lysander's hands.

'Your father would have been proud of you today,' he said with a tight smile.

As the horse thundered back towards the barracks, the Fire of Ares knocked against Lysander's chest. The pendant felt more like a curse than a talisman. It was the symbol of his ties not only to his father, but to Sparta. A place that thrived on the blood and sweat of Helot slaves.

The other boys at the barracks were lined up outside. They must have been told what had happened. Lysander dismounted and made his way towards the entrance, head bowed.

'Welcome back Lysander!' shouted Diokles. 'The Earth Goddess was thirsty for Helot blood, and he poured her a fine offering tonight.'

Lysander felt his fists clench, but he didn't look back. A few of the boys slapped him on the back, murmuring words of encouragement.

Orpheus alone, leaning heavily on his stick, stepped out of the crowd. He hobbled forward and placed a hand on Lysander's shoulder.

'Are you all right, Lysander?'

He stopped and faced his friend.

'Haven't you heard? I'm one of you now. A true Spartan.'

Lysander turned and walked inside.

CHAPTER 3

'You have to eat, Lysander,' said Orpheus as they sat in the main hall of the barracks at the long table. Boys along the benches on either side were chattering through mouthfuls of food. A handful of Helot slaves waited patiently along the wall, ready to receive instructions. Lysander's friend, Leonidas, looked up from his food – he hadn't spoken to Lysander all day. *He probably doesn't know what to say*, Lysander thought. Leonidas was the second son of one of Sparta's two Kings. Only the first-born was spared the agoge, the barracks upbringing.

Lysander stared at the bowl of lentils in front of him. He had washed the dried blood from his face and hands several times since that morning. Even after the water ran clear, he still felt stained.

'Those Helots deserved what they got,' said Prokles from further down the table. 'We couldn't let them go unpunished.' Others nodded in agreement.

'I wish I had been there,' said Ariston. 'Diokles says

the streets ran with blood.' A fist of guilt closed tightly over Lysander's heart. He felt sickened by what he'd done to his friend.

'You had to do it,' said Leonidas from across the table – quietly, so that his voice would pass unheeded beneath the din. 'If the whip hadn't been in your hand, one of the Krypteia would have lashed Timeon. And harder too.'

This didn't make Lysander feel much better. It sounded like a coward's argument. Lysander still had doubts about the prince's bravery. After all, Leonidas hadn't come to Lysander's aid when the Krypteia dragged him from his bed.

'Have you heard any news of him?' Lysander asked softly.

Neither of his friends answered, so he reached across the table and laid a hand on the prince's arm.

'Leonidas, is Timeon recovering?'

Leonidas swallowed and eventually looked Lysander in the eye.

'The word among the Helots is that he's being cared for at the settlement by his family. They won't say much more.' Leonidas paused. 'It doesn't look good.'

A groan escaped Lysander's lips, and he buried his head in his hands.

'You should go and visit him, Lysander,' Orpheus said. 'We can make excuses for you with Diokles.'

Lysander swallowed back tears, and looked up at Orpheus. *What's stopping me?* he asked himself.

21

Timeon's my oldest friend.

'You're right!' he said. 'I will go. I'll tell him how sorry I am, explain that I had no choice . . .'

Even as he spoke, Lysander imagined Timeon's wounds, leaking blood through whatever dirty dressings his mother had found. He pictured the look of betrayal in his friend's eyes. Lysander's confidence evaporated.

'I can't . . .' he said. 'Not yet.'

'The sooner you go and see him, the better you'll both feel,' said Orpheus.

Lysander knew it was true, but the thought of seeing Timeon terrified him. His guilt rested on his shoulders like a yoke, and he didn't have the strength to throw it off. There was more to courage than facing your enemies. Facing your friends could be worse.

He pushed his wooden dish away. Climbing over the bench he walked towards the door. Diokles stepped into the room and barred his path.

'Our punisher!' he said loudly, a smile spreading across his face. 'Your right arm did Sparta proud this morning.'

A few boys cheered, and Diokles continued. 'Take your seats, everyone. I have news.'

Lysander reluctantly returned to the bench beside Orpheus. He heard the boy called Hilarion whisper, 'What's happening?' No one ventured an answer.

Diokles stood at the top of the table, leaning his weight on his massive fists. The tutor's dark beard was freshly trimmed, but his eye patch was the same piece of brown leather as always. He stared at them with his one good eye as they settled.

'Sparta is the greatest State in Greece, and her men are the strongest. That is why we take you from your parents at seven years. Not like those chubby Athenians who grow up in their mothers' bosoms, learning to sew clothes. You boys have been in Spartan training for six years now. Some – the weak – have died. Their deaths are testament to your will and determination. Now it is time for you to become young men. You must prove yourselves in the mountains.'

Lysander felt the hairs on the back of his neck stiffen.

'You will be sent into the Taygetos Mountains in pairs,' boomed Diokles, his eyes scanning the boys. 'There you must survive for five nights using only your wits, your strength and your will. They say the snows are coming early this year, and icy winds blow from the north. Food is scarce. You will drink from the rivers and eat only what you can catch with your bare hands.' He looked towards the doorway. 'Solon! Enter!'

Lysander turned with the others as a stocky young man entered. He wore a red cloak and limped forward. His black hair was short and tightly curled. A deep pink scar ran down from his forehead, over his closed left eye. Half of his nose was torn away, and his top lip forked in two. His front teeth were missing as well.

'Solon is approaching the age of manhood,' said

Diokles. 'The injuries you see were suffered on his Ordeal five summers ago. Tell them, Solon.'

The visitor stepped forward beside Diokles.

'I was looking for food when it happened.' His voice was slurred because of his disfigurement. 'It was the fourth day, and I was in the forest when I heard what sounded like a puppy mewling. I followed the sound until I came to a tree. There was a hollow in the base of the trunk and, as I peered closer, I could see animals squirming in the darkness. You get so hungry in the mountains, you'll eat anything: leaves, moss, even the bark from trees. I fell to my knees and thrust my hand into the hole. I grabbed one of the creatures by the hind legs and pulled it out: a fat little piglet. Hunger drove me wild – I couldn't wait to skewer the tender meat over a fire. I would have eaten it still dripping with blood. Then I heard another noise behind me, and pain ripped through my leg. I turned to see a huge sow with sharp yellow tusks. Her teeth had gone through my ankle tendon as though it were soft cheese. Then she came for my face.' Lysander heard a whimper from among the students. 'That's the last thing I remember.'

Lysander's heart was beating fast, and he felt sick.

'Leave us, Solon,' said Diokles. 'And bear your injuries with pride, like a true Spartan.' Solon gave a small bow and left. The students were silent, their faces pale.

'You will live like animals,' said Diokles. 'There are dangers besides wild beasts that can tear you apart:

loose rocky cliffs, bitter cold, poisonous plants. This is the test of a Spartan.' Diokles stared straight at Lysander. 'Those who are weak and do not pass, shame their families by their failure and death.'

The door to the dining hall creaked open. It was Sarpedon! Lysander had not seen his grandfather since the awful night of the Festival Games, when the old man had been humiliated at the hands of the Helots. Lysander remembered Sarpedon on his knees, bleeding from a cut to his head, his grey hair dishevelled and his tunic torn. Only his eyes had retained their dignity, showing no fear of the blade that was held to his throat by his own treacherous slave, Strabo.

Now he stood with his shoulders pulled back, the tallest man in the room, with his red cloak immaculate and his silver hair carefully tied back. Lysander smiled, but his grandfather did not acknowledge the greeting. What could Lysander expect? Sarpedon was an Ephor, one of the most powerful men in Sparta. Far too important to acknowledge a grandson. His duty to the State came before any love for his family.

Diokles gave a shallow bow of the head as Sarpedon greeted him, then he stepped back to allow the Ephor to address the room.

'Spartans,' Sarpedon began in his deep, gravelled tones. 'Your tutor has told you it is time to face the Ordeal. Before the next full moon, you will all be tested, but I am here to select the first pairing to enter the wilderness.'

A low murmuring passed along the table.

'Who do you think it will be?' Hilarion asked his neighbour. 'I hope it's not . . .'

'Quiet!' boomed Sarpedon.

Lysander was sure he would not be chosen. It was a great honour to be picked first, and surely Sarpedon couldn't be seen to choose his own grandson for such a privilege.

'The first two,' said Sarpedon, 'will be the winners at the Festival Games, Lysander and Demaratos.'

Everyone in the room gasped. All the other students looked at Lysander with a mixture of amazement and envy. All apart from one. Standing between Ariston and Prokles, and taller by a handspan, Demaratos stared at him with unconcealed hatred. His eyes were as black as his cropped hair.

'How could they pair me with my hated enemy?' Lysander muttered under his breath. Since the night of the Games, they had barely spoken. Demaratos's dislocated shoulder had been slow to heal, and he massaged it now, all the time holding Lysander's gaze. He had fallen awkwardly during their wrestling match at the Games, and had been forced to withdraw. Demaratos could not forgive Lysander for this injury. Lysander could not forgive Demaratos for stealing the Fire of Ares, when he and his cronies had attacked Lysander in a side street.

'But . . .' Demaratos stood up and started to object.

'Silence!' shouted Diokles. 'How dare you interrupt an Ephor!'

26

Demaratos shrank back beside Prokles and Ariston. Sarpedon continued.

'The winners of the Games will be rewarded with five days' rest in the mountains,' he smiled. 'Don't fear. You will not be alone. Each pair is accompanied by one of the *ephebes*, who will make sure life is not too . . . leisurely.'

Lysander had forgotten that there would be an older boy with them. An *ephebos* was the name given to a student on the cusp of manhood, one who had reached eighteen years.

'Demaratos and Lysander will be guided by Agesilaus.' The name meant nothing to Lysander. 'Enter!'

A heavy-set young man walked into the room and took his place beside Sarpedon. His appearance was unusual for a Spartan. His hair was pale yellow, almost white, and his eyes were vivid green like a cat's. One of his forearms was covered with scar tissue, pink, shiny and hairless. Lysander had spotted him once or twice before, training with the older boys from a nearby barracks. He didn't speak, but his eyes gazed out at Lysander with cold ferocity. Lysander suppressed a shiver.

'Fetch your cloaks,' said Sarpedon, 'and gather outside.'

His grandfather turned and strode out of the room with Agesilaus following close behind. The students scrambled from their seats and poured through the door. As he was leaving, Lysander heard Demaratos speaking with Diokles.

'How can I go into the mountains?' he said under his breath. 'My shoulder – it isn't properly healed.' He pulled aside his tunic. A pale green bruise still covered the area where the joint had become dislocated.

'It is called the Ordeal, because you must suffer,' said Diokles coldly. 'There will be no special treatment.' As Lysander walked past, Demaratos gave him an icy stare. 'If you're lucky, you'll escape with your lives. If not, you deserved to die anyway.'

In the dormitory, Orpheus held out a hemp sack to Lysander.

'Make sure you take a blanket – it'll be freezing up there,' he said.

'They won't let you take a blanket,' sneered Demaratos from across the room. 'You take your cloak, and that's it. No weapons, no food.'

Nevertheless, Lysander opened the wooden chest beside his bed, and took out his sling. He dropped it into the sack, along with a thin blanket, the only one he had.

'Take this as well,' said Leonidas, reaching into his own box. He offered Lysander a leather pouch. Inside were two stones.

'What are these?' asked Lysander.

'One's a flint,' said Leonidas. 'The other is a stone containing iron. Striking the flint on the stone will create a spark. Hopefully, there'll be some dry tinder in the mountain to light a fire.'

28

'Thanks,' said Lysander. 'I still can't believe Sarpedon picked me.'

'The Gods are smiling on you,' said his friend. 'I was praying the Ephor would choose me.'

'You'll have your chance,' said Lysander. He wanted to say more, but there was a commotion further down the room. A few of the boys had gathered at the end of the dormitory, where the joker of the barracks, Hilarion, was talking.

'Have you heard the stories about Agesilaus?' said Hilarion loudly. 'I can tell you a true story about Agesilaus and his brother Nisos.' Lysander gathered his cloak around his shoulders and joined the back of the group. Everyone was listening to Hilarion's tale. 'In a barracks tournament one year, the brothers were drawn against each other in a wrestling match. Their father was one of the Council, and told them both to make him proud. The match was long and violent. Neither wanted to admit defeat. Nisos broke Agesilaus' ankle, but he fought on. Finally Agesilaus managed to get a stranglehold on his brother as they lay grappling on the ground.'

'What sort of hold?' asked Prokles.

'I'll show you,' said Hilarion. He pulled Prokles towards him. 'Sit down.'

Prokles was grinning and did as he was told. Hilarion sat behind him, and wrapped both legs around Prokles' waist. He looped his arm around Prokles' neck and leant backwards.

'He wouldn't let go,' said Hilarion, as Prokles' hands began to flail and claw at him. 'When Nisos' face started to turn purple, the referee tried to stop the contest, but Agesilaus held firm.' Prokles' face was turning red. His smile had turned to a grimace as he fought for breath. 'Eventually, the referee had to strike Agesilaus several times on the back with his rod before he finally released his brother.' Hilarion let go of Prokles, who immediately threw himself at the story-teller. Everyone was laughing at the spectacle, and even Lysander smiled. Demaratos and Ariston managed to pull Prokles off the smaller boy.

'You could have killed me!' Prokles shouted.

'You asked,' grinned Hilarion.

'Enough,' said Demaratos. 'Tell us what happened to Nisos.'

'He was lying face down on the ground,' said Hilarion quietly. 'When they turned him over, there was a lot of blood. The vessels in his nose and eyes had burst. He died there in the dirt. Agesilaus turned away from his brother and went to accept his prize.'

The boys fell silent. Orpheus was first to speak up.

'And what about Agesilaus? Was he punished?'

'After Nisos had been carried away,' said Hilarion, 'Agesilaus' father approached his son, his face unreadable. Many thought he would slay his son on the spot. He looked down at Nisos' blood in the dust, and then placed his hands either side of Agesilaus' face to look him in the eye.'

'And?' said Prokles.

'He said, "I see I have raised at least one good son" and walked away.'

'Is that all?' exclaimed Prokles.

'That's all he said,' replied Hilarion.

Lysander turned away from the group. He tucked the Fire of Ares into his tunic and walked out of the dormitory carrying his sack. He didn't look back. Lysander was about to go into the mountains with his enemy, Demaratos, and another boy who was a monster. He was to fight for his life, flanked on either side by two people he couldn't trust. And back in the Helot settlement, his oldest friend lay with flesh ripped apart by Lysander's own hand. As he stepped outside, he looked up at the mountains that loomed to the west.

'If the Gods help me,' he muttered, 'it's more than I deserve.'

CHAPTER 4

'Hurry up!' ordered Diokles.

Lysander left through the barracks gates, carrying only the canvas sack that hung from his shoulder by a cord. Leonidas and Orpheus came behind him, and the other students followed in a trickle. On the road beyond, which would take them west to the Taygetos Mountains, Sarpedon was waiting. He held the reins of Pegasus, his horse. The stallion swished his tail against his black flanks to ward off flies.

Lysander was surprised to see Kassandra standing beside her grandfather. She was wrapped in a thick woollen sheath dress, embroidered with silver flowers. The breeze ruffled her hair, which hung loosely tied with a gilt clasp. Lysander had thought of his cousin often since the night of the Games, and each time the memory sparked his anger. He had trusted her, but all along she had been meeting Demaratos secretly. He wouldn't be so naive again. At his approach, her gaze fell to the ground.

Sarpedon beckoned Lysander aside. They walked a few paces away from the crowd.

'I hope that you appreciate the honour I have shown you, Lysander.'

His grandfather's face was unreadable.

'Yes,' said Lysander, 'but why must I go with Demaratos? We hate one another.'

'Listen, my grandson, no man in a red cloak is your enemy. You must learn that. And besides, it will be good for you to leave Sparta for a while,' he said. He looked over the top of Lysander's head, straight at Diokles. 'Away from . . . influences.'

'What influences?'

Sarpedon's face became grave, and he placed a hand on Lysander's arm.

'You must understand: the Elders are still nervous after the Festival Games,' he said. 'They are embarrassed that a mothax like you was all that stood between the Helots and rebellion. Some even suggest that you were responsible.'

'But I saved them,' protested Lysander. He was suddenly angry. 'And you lied to me. They came after the Helots. They made me lash Timeon.'

For a moment Sarpedon's grip on his arm tightened, and Lysander was afraid.

'Of course they did,' said his grandfather. 'I am one man, Lysander. And Sparta is made up of many men. That is what makes us great. Don't forget the honour I have given you by placing you in the agoge.

Timeon is not important.'

'He's my best friend!' said Lysander.

Sarpedon's expression didn't change.

'Timeon was as guilty as the others on that terrible night. His punishment was deserved.'

'Timeon has lived as a slave his entire life,' Lysander argued. 'You could never understand.'

When Sarpedon spoke again, his voice was softer.

'Perhaps not. But there are protocols that must be followed. Do you think I spared the whip on Strabo?'

'You found him?' asked Lysander in amazement. The last time he had seen Sarpedon's treacherous slave, he was running from the Temple of Ortheia in fear, having threatened his master's life. Sarpedon jerked his head towards his stallion. Lysander spotted a figure clutching the reins. Strabo. His back was hunched and he looked afraid. A scar extended up his cheek and above his eyebrow, making one eyelid droop in the corner.

'He came back to me in the end,' said Sarpedon. 'He begged forgiveness for his treachery and insolence. I made sure he knew the price of that mercy.'

'Assemble yourselves in marching order,' shouted Diokles. 'Three columns.'

As the boys jostled into position, Lysander stared at the cowed, twisted figure by the horse. Whatever fire had been in Strabo's heart was clearly extinguished. Sarpedon had once granted Strabo his freedom and employed him as head of his household, but now he was nothing but a slave again, with a life of hard toil ahead.

'Anyway,' said Sarpedon, 'there were other reasons for the mass punishment. We cannot risk another uprising, not now . . .' His words trailed off. 'Take your place in the line.' Lysander's grandfather seemed to hesitate, before continuing. 'The Ordeal is hard. It is harder still if you don't have courage. Remember all you have learnt, obey Agesilaus, and work together. No boy can face the Ordeal on his own. You will need your compatriots. May the Gods watch over you all.'

Lysander nodded, but Sarpedon had already turned back to Pegasus.

'Hurry up!' shouted Diokles. 'The mountains will wait for ever, but I will not.'

Lysander took his place at the rear of the line – he didn't want to march with Demaratos. He needed time to think.

As he swung his bag over his shoulder, Kassandra appeared at his side.

'What do you want?' said Lysander, keeping his eyes straight ahead.

'I wanted . . . I came to say thank you,' she said. 'You saved my grandfather's life on the night of the Festival Games.' She reached out a hand and her fingers brushed Lysander's arm. 'You saved my life too.' Lysander pulled away.

'March!' ordered Diokles from the front. The columns moved off in unison. Lysander was glad to leave Kassandra behind. But then she was by his side again, jogging to keep up with the pace of the students.

'Why don't you go and trot along next to Demaratos,' said Lysander. 'You and he are together, aren't you?'

Kassandra was breathing heavily and spoke in a rush.

'Demaratos's family and my own have been close for many generations. My mother was a cousin of his father. That's how Spartan hierarchies work. I must be civil with Demaratos. It is the Spartan tradition.'

'I'm tired of Spartan tradition,' said Lysander. 'It seems to be an excuse to treat others badly.'

'The choice isn't mine to make,' said Kassandra. 'I've lived my whole life knowing that I'll one day be married to Demaratos.'

Lysander snorted. 'But do you care for him, too?'

Kassandra sighed, and shot a glance back towards where Sarpedon was waiting.

'He's better than you think,' she said. 'He fears you, that's all.'

Fears me? thought Lysander. She couldn't know how awful Demaratos really was in the barracks. She couldn't see his arrogance.

'Look —' she was panting now. 'Take this.' Lysander felt a bag pushed into his hand. 'It's dried meat,' said his cousin. The gift took Lysander by surprise. It was a simple leather pouch tied with a piece of twine.

'We aren't allowed anything but bread,' he said.

'Please, take it. It might just save your life.'

Reluctantly, Lysander loosened the mouth of his sack and slipped the pouch inside. He started to thank his cousin, but she was no longer by his side. Lysander looked round and saw she had slowed to a walk. Her eyes pleaded with him.

She wants to know that I've forgiven her, he thought to himself. *Very well.* Lysander nodded once, then turned back to his march. The dust swirled around his shoulders. When he looked round a second time, she had gone.

They marched through the middle of the day. A few of the boys had grumbled, but Diokles insisted it was good training for warfare. 'The heat of the autumn sun doesn't dictate to Spartans!' he'd said.

They took the road between the Spartan villages of Kynosaura and Mesoa, passing the huge single-storey barracks and dining messes where Spartan men lived and trained. The mountains, tinged blue in the distance, were tipped with white snow.

As they marched past a series of carpentry workshops a low thundering came from up ahead.

'Off the road!' commanded Diokles from the front of the columns.

Around the corner appeared a squadron of red-cloaked soldiers, carrying shields and spears held vertically. The men held their shoulders back and Lysander could see the muscles that bulged in their arms from a lifetime's training. Lysander broke ranks with the other boys and scattered out of the way as the soldiers charged past. They left the air heavy with dust clouds and the smell of stale sweat. It was a sight Lysander and the others saw every day outside the barracks – a reminder of the mighty Spartan army. A reminder also of Lysander's future: he would live in barracks as a soldier until the age of thirty.

Leaving the villages behind, they were soon surrounded by Spartan farmland. The boys threaded their way between the low, filthy Helot settlements, where the smells of human waste mingled with that of the animals that lived around them. Lysander had left his life of poverty, but he knew that for the rest of the Helots there was no hope of escape.

It was late into the afternoon by the time the boys reached the foothills of the mountains, where shepherds' paths cut through the low undergrowth up into the hills. They hadn't eaten all day, and Lysander felt a hollow ache in his stomach.

'Halt!' ordered Diokles.

The boys fell out of line. The tutor glanced towards the mountains. The sky was clear. He stood before Demaratos and Lysander with Agesilaus by his side, his green eyes twinkling with malevolence.

'Let me check your sacks,' said Diokles. 'No food is permitted besides a ration of bread.'

Demaratos handed his sack to Diokles, Agesilaus took Lysander's. As the bags were searched, Lysander willed the older boy not to see the pouch of meat. But how could he miss it? Eventually, Agesilaus sneered and pulled out Lysander's leather sling.

'What's this?' he said.

Diokles peered over.

'A reminder from his days as a Helot, I think!'

'The wolves will be afraid,' joked Agesilaus. He dropped the sling back in Lysander's bag. The meat was safe.

Diokles took down three water flasks that hung from his shoulder. One was smaller than the others, and he gave this one to Agesilaus.

'Don't waste this,' said the tutor. 'Keep it until you are desperate. Agesilaus is used to the Ordeal, so he won't need as much.'

The older boy smiled.

'It is time to say your farewells, Spartans,' said Diokles. 'Agesilaus is your leader up there. Obey him, or face my wrath.'

Lysander turned to see the other students watching them. All faces were serious.

Lysander looked away. He didn't want the Gods to be on his side. The need to punish himself for what he had done to Timeon was overwhelming. The image of his friend's bloodied back flashed into Lysander's mind. He hurried over to Leonidas.

'I wish you good luck,' said Leonidas.

'Friend, I'd like you to do something for me,' Lysander said.

'Anything,' replied Leonidas.

Lysander lifted the leather thong from around his

neck. The red stone of the Fire of Ares glimmered. He held it out to Leonidas.

'Give this to Timeon. He knows what it means to me. Tell him I'm truly sorry.'

Leonidas gripped the pendant and gave a quick nod.

'Enough!' shouted Diokles. 'It's time to face the Ordeal.'

Lysander stepped forward with Demaratos.

'Are you ready?' asked the tutor.

Agesilaus held out his fist between them and stared at Demaratos. He clenched his hand and brought it down to rest on top of the older boy's. Now they both switched their gazes to Lysander. Reluctantly, he curled his own hand into a fist and placed it on top of Demaratos's. The crowd of boys gave a massive cheer.

'One more thing,' said Diokles. 'Your cloaks – hand them over.'

'What?' said Demaratos. 'It's freezing in the mountains.'

'Take them off!' shouted Diokles.

Lysander obeyed, unhooking his cloak and handing it to the tutor. He felt vulnerable without the wool next to his skin. Demaratos did the same. Lysander could see wisps of cloud streaking the peaks above. Though the sun was shining now, it would be bitterly cold once it fell below the horizon.

'Follow me,' ordered Agesilaus, turning to face the steep climb into the hills. Lysander took a last look at the other students, and then fell into step behind their guide.

Will I ever see my barracks again? he wondered. The boys behind them called out good luck and Lysander raised a hand in farewell without looking back.

His future lay in the mountains.

Agesilaus led the way up the path. Lysander did his best to keep up, despite the burning in his calves. He could hear Demaratos breathing heavily with the effort of climbing. The other boy's body leant slightly to one side as he heaved himself up the mountainside and Lysander realised that his recent shoulder injury must already be making things difficult for him.

The slope became steeper. Finally, they reached a small ridge, where Agesilaus took a sip from his flask. *I'll save mine*, thought Lysander. He had no idea how thirsty he might get over the coming days and it was too early to start using up his precious supplies. Looking back down the mountain, he could see Diokles and the neat rows of Spartans, no more than red specks now, marching back to the barracks. Dusk was approaching, and the wind had picked up, gusting down the mountainside. The sweat on Lysander's back made him shiver.

'We should find some shelter,' said Lysander. 'Before it gets too dark.'

'Shut your mouth, Helot,' said Agesilaus. 'I'm leading this group.'

Demaratos turned and smirked.

They climbed higher as night fell. Lysander could feel blisters forming across his toes, making his foot throb with every step. The wind was constant, numbing the side of his face. He placed his hands under his armpits to try and warm them.

Agesilaus stopped ahead. 'That's far enough for today.' He pointed to a shallow dip between several hills. Stunted olive trees formed a small copse. 'Let's rest down there, under those trees. It will be out of the wind.'

'When do we eat?' asked Lysander as they descended from the ridge.

'Can't you last half a day without food?' sneered Demaratos. 'You're pathetic!'

'You're the one stuffing your face in the dining hall every day,' replied Lysander.

'Quiet, you two!' yelled Agesilaus. 'It's too late to hunt. We'll find some food at sunrise.'

To Lysander's relief, the small olive grove was sheltered from the wind, though the piercing cold of night was already working its way into his bones.

'Shall we light a fire?' he asked. He had a flint in his sack, and there was plenty of tinder about.

'We'll manage without,' said Agesilaus. 'The flames will attract wild animals.'

'You know nothing,' Demaratos told Lysander. 'You'll get us all killed before the Ordeal has even started.'

'Neither of you know anything,' corrected Agesilaus. Demaratos's smile slipped away. 'You think life in the barracks is hard? You wait: the Ordeal is ten times as bad. You'll be so hungry soon that you'd chew the leather of your sandals.'

Lysander thought of the meat in his sack – he'd save that for when he was truly desperate.

'Your bones will feel cold enough to shatter like ice,' said Agesilaus. 'I've been here before, I know.'

'We should try to build a shelter,' said Lysander.

Agesilaus snorted.

'You really are hopeless. What are you going to build this shelter with?'

Lysander looked around. Agesilaus was right. Besides a few fragments of dead wood, there was nothing.

The older boy scrambled up a gnarled olive tree, settling into a natural seat where the branches sprouted from the trunk.

'At least I'll still be alive in the morning,' he sneered. 'Nothing can get me up here.'

Lysander saw another tree with a hollow and darted over to it, but Demaratos got there first and pulled himself up into the branches.

'This one's mine, half-breed. Find another.'

Lysander walked some distance away, but no other trees were suitable. In the end he sat at the base of a trunk and hugged his knees to his chest. He'd never felt so alone.

Night fell swiftly, and the colour of the landscape

leached away as the sky faded from dark blue to black. Noises started gradually. First it was only a rustle, making Lysander sit up, alert. Then sounds came from all around. It was impossible to tell where any of the noises were coming from or how far away they were. Was that whispering? *Don't be foolish!* he scolded himself. *It's only the wind in the trees.*

A howl echoed through the hills. Wolves! Would they attack? A second howl sounded out and Lysander picked up a branch of wood that he could use as a makeshift club. If wild animals did lurk in the darkness, he would be ready for them. He set his back against the trunk and waited. He could hear Demaratos snoring softly, safe among the branches of his tree.

Lysander's first night in the mountains was going to be a long one.

He hoped he'd survive to see the dawn.

CHAPTER 5

Lysander woke with a shiver. Would his nightmares ever stop? He had dreamt about his mother again last night and the pain in his heart only seemed to get worse each time her face returned in his sleep.

The stars had vanished, masked by grey clouds. The hills rose above him menacingly, shrouded in dark shadows. The bare olive trees looked like twisted skeletons. It was achingly cold. Peering through the darkness, he could make out Demaratos's huddled form. He was shivering too. Agesilaus was still cradled in the branches of his tree and, from the tilt of his head, appeared fast asleep. Lysander rubbed his arms and legs, trying to encourage some warmth to flow through them. He closed his eyes and tried to imagine his thick cloak wrapped around him. It was no use. The cold had lodged in his bones.

He had to find some warmth soon. Despite the weariness in his limbs, Lysander stood up and circled his arms.

'What are you doing?' said Demaratos from where he was huddled.

'Trying to get warm,' said Lysander.

'Well, do it somewhere else,' said Demaratos. 'I'm trying to sleep.'

Lysander made his way up the far edge of the hollow, where an ancient tree stump jutted out of the ground. The middle had rotted away, leaving a space just big enough to crouch inside. It was filled with damp leaves and what looked like the decomposed skeleton of a bird. But it was better than nothing and Lysander climbed inside. With his knees up against his chest, only his head and shoulders protruded from the top. It was uncomfortable and smelled fetid, but at least it would shelter most of his body from the wind. His hands and feet were tingling. Lysander rested his head against the bark and closed his eyes.

'Get up, you two,' shouted Agesilaus.

Lysander climbed stiffly from his shelter. Dawn light crept into the hollow between the hills, and a thin mist hung in the air. He stretched his arms above his head as Demaratos yawned and sat up. Agesilaus was thirty paces away by a clump of bushes.

'You two are hopeless,' he shouted. 'The birds will have the best berries soon.'

Berries! Lysander ran over, his muscles screaming, to where Agesilaus was picking the fruit. Demaratos stumbled beside him.

'Get out of my way!' Demaratos snarled, tearing at the red fruit, and stuffing it into his mouth. Anger coursed through Lysander. He rushed at his enemy, and shoved him to the ground. Lysander reached past him, lunging at another clump of berries.

'You monster!' he shouted at Demaratos. Hunger had reduced Lysander to this – to squabbling in the dirt over berries.

Agesilaus came forward and aimed a fierce kick at Lysander's shoulder, throwing him on top of Demaratos. The two of them sprawled in the dirt.

'It's time to go. Gather your things.'

Demaratos stood up, his fingers stained red.

'Delicious,' he said, wiping his mouth.

Lysander climbed to his feet. He'd have to be quicker if he was going to survive.

They gathered their sacks and hurried after Agesilaus, who was already picking his way up a small rock face.

'Where are we going?' asked Demaratos.

'We have to get further south,' said Agesilaus. 'Deeper into mountain territory. There are more animals to hunt, and rivers too. That's where the challenge really starts.'

Lysander had only just made it through the first night. Now he was being told things were going to get worse. *Can I do this?* he thought. What if he failed? He watched the two other boys as they heaved themselves up the rocks. He had no choice; he had to follow. He only hoped he'd survive.

The mist soon burned away and was replaced by bright sunlight. Agesilaus led the way across ridges and into shallow valleys, but the streambeds were all dry. Lysander fought the urge to quench his thirst from his precious supply of water. He saw Agesilaus picking the leaves off plants as they went and sucking them. Lysander did the same. Each droplet of dew on his parched tongue tasted divine. They gradually climbed higher.

As the sun reached its highest point in the sky, they skirted the edge of a small mound. Lysander was feeling light-headed and stumbled and fell.

'On your feet!' shouted Agesilaus. Lysander climbed dizzily to his knees. He felt weak through lack of food. Agesilaus walked past him, up the hill. Demaratos followed him, pausing only to spit into the dirt by Lysander's grazed hands. A movement behind a shrub further down the slope caught Lysander's eye. Still in a crouch, he crept over. There, beside the bush, he could see the white of a rabbit's tail.

Up ahead, Demaratos skidded on some loose rocks that clattered down the hill. The rabbit darted away, then paused when it was only twenty paces from Lysander, lifting its nose to sniff the air.

Lysander reached slowly for his sling. The thought of the grilled flesh flooded his mouth with saliva.

'You'll never hit it with that,' came a voice. Lysander looked over his shoulder; Demaratos had made his way back to join him. Lysander could hear the desperation in the other boy's voice and he could see how closely Demaratos was watching the rabbit. *He needs food as much as I do*, Lysander reminded himself.

With the sling in one hand, and keeping his eyes on the rabbit, Lysander felt blindly on the ground for a stone. After some scrabbling he found one that fitted perfectly between his index finger and thumb. The rabbit hadn't moved. Lysander crept forward, holding both ends of the leather strap in one hand so it dangled in a loop. He balanced the stone carefully in the centre of the loop, and began to swing the strap around, quickly so that the stone didn't fall out. Still the rabbit did not flee. It was too busy nibbling grass.

Lysander stood up slowly. He felt the light breeze in his face: he was downwind. As long as the rabbit didn't turn in his direction, he'd be fine. He remembered all the time in the fields when he and Timeon used to aim at crows. He swung the strap faster and faster, lifting it steadily above his head. Then he released.

As the stone struck the rabbit, it took an awkward jump, then fell to the ground, legs twitching.

'Yes!' shouted Lysander jubilantly. There was a scramble of feet, and Lysander turned to see Agesilaus striding towards him.

'I didn't say you could stop!' he shouted.

'We've got a rabbit!' said Demaratos. *We?* Lysander thought. But he was too hungry to protest. He ran forward to claim his prize.

Blood oozed from behind the wild animal's ear. A direct hit. Now he would skin it, gut it and place the carcass over a fire. Soon he would be tearing tender meat off the bones.

Agesilaus shoved him out of the way and peered at the body.

'You can't eat that,' he said with contempt.

'Why not?' asked Lysander.

'It's riddled with disease,' said Agesilaus. He leant down and picked up the rabbit by the scruff of its neck, then held it in front of Lysander's face. Sure enough, the rabbit's eyes were milky and infected, and there were ticks nestled in the matted fur. Agesilaus threw the body at Lysander's feet and stalked off.

'Enough time-wasting,' he said. 'Let's go!'

'You can't do anything right,' said Demaratos. 'We'd all be dead if we'd eaten that.' He strode after Agesilaus.

Lysander gazed down at the rabbit, feeling hungrier than ever.

'My stomach feels bad,' said Demaratos. They were moving out of a small copse of pine trees, on to a slope of rocky ground covered in low bushes and shrubs.

'It's probably all the berries you ate,' said Lysander. 'They weren't ripe.'

'How would you know?' said Demaratos, shooting him a look of hatred.

'They should fall off the plant easily,' said Lysander. 'You tore into them.'

'We can shelter over there,' said Agesilaus, pointing across to a dip in the mountainside. 'It'll be safe from predators.'

Lysander could see the spot he meant. A huge cliff rose from the ground forming an overhang above a small flat clearing. They were separated from it by a treacherous-looking slope of loose gravel.

'If we get there,' said Agesilaus, 'it will be safe to light a fire. Otherwise, we'll have to push on.'

That decided it for Lysander. He didn't think he could take another night in the cold.

'Lysander goes first,' said Agesilaus. 'He can test how loose the gravel is underfoot.'

'He won't dare,' said Demaratos.

Lysander pushed past the two of them. *I'll show them I'm not a coward*, he thought.

Lysander stepped on to the gravel, his hand balancing him against the slope. His foot slid, sending a shower of flint below. His heart jumped into his throat as he watched the pebbles bounce and hurtle out of sight. He forced himself to take another step. More gravel skittered down the sheer slope, disappearing over the cliff edge to hurtle through empty air. Lysander couldn't be sure that the next step wouldn't send him sliding to his death. Sweat sprang out on his brow and he had to concentrate hard not to give in to the panic that he could feel pushing from the back of his mind. He willed himself to take one step and then another until slowly, slowly hope began to replace fear. He'd made it! Lysander let out a whoop of exultation as he arrived on solid ground at the other side.

'I did it!' he shouted back to the others.

Now it was Demaratos's turn. Lysander could see he looked pale and how the other boy's hands trembled as he put them out to steady himself. He came sideways like a crab, facing the slope so that he could hold on with both hands in case he slipped. Once both his feet were on the solid ground, he turned to Lysander. He passed a hand over his face to mask the tic that had started up in one of his eyes.

'You took ages,' he sneered. 'I don't know why you made a fuss.' Lysander didn't say a word. He didn't have to. He simply allowed his gaze to rest on the tic in Demaratos's eye. The other boy turned away, cursing quietly under his breath.

Agesilaus ran across, each foot sending flint cascading below. His bravery and skill were extraordinary and Lysander felt shame flush his face. The older boy made it look so easy.

'You two collect firewood,' said Agesilaus, 'and I'll gather stones for a hearth.' He wasn't even out of breath.

But Demaratos had fallen to his knees and was holding his belly.

'I don't think I can help,' he moaned. 'My stomach keeps cramping up.' He lifted his tunic, and Lysander could see that the skin across his midriff was bloated and tight as a drum. A sheen of sweat had broken out across his forehead.

'You fool,' said Agesilaus. 'How could you eat unripe fruit? Are you such a victim of hunger?'

Demaratos groaned again. 'You have to help me.'

Lysander spotted a distant copse of pine trees. Perhaps peppermint would be growing there? It'd help to calm Demaratos's stomach. He climbed to his feet and set off down the hillside.

'Where are you going?' asked Agesilaus.

'I'm going to find something to help him,' he said to Agesilaus. 'If we're going to survive up here, we all need to be healthy.'

Lysander moved swiftly down the slope. Looking back towards the plains, he could pick out three of the five villages of Sparta, loosely linked by tracks that extended into the surrounding fields. The acropolis, the low hill that housed the Temple of the Goddess Athena and the Council House, stood at the centre.

Lysander soon reached the copse of pine trees. He could smell mint and found a few plants sprouting at the base of the trees. He set about gathering the bright green leaves. He was soon out of breath – the mountain air was thin – and he paused to sit among the pine cones.

A harsh cry overhead made him look up. Circling high above the treetops was an eagle. Lysander could pick out the fanned feathers on its wing tips as it soared majestically on the currents of air. *Looking for prey*, Lysander thought. This made him remember Kassandra's gift – the meat in his sack.

Lysander took out the pouch. He untied the length of twine, and pulled out a crispy strip of dried pork. He lifted the precious meat to his lips and he could feel his mouth fill with saliva.

A twig snapped behind him.

Lysander was pushed to the ground. Someone gripped his arm and twisted it up behind his back. Another hand grabbed his hair and yanked his head backwards. Pain seared through his shoulders as his wrists were pushed higher.

'I thought you'd been gone too long,' hissed Agesilaus in his ear. 'Did you get lost?'

'Let go of me,' said Lysander and tried to squirm away, but the older boy's grip was firm. He pushed Lysander to the ground. With his free hand he grabbed the pouch containing the meat. Sprigs of peppermint were ground into the dirt by Lysander's face. Agesilaus let go of Lysander to open the pouch. He peered inside it and a look of fury flashed through his eyes. Then he smiled.

'It looks as though you've been keeping a little secret, doesn't it? Did you think I wouldn't find out?'

'That's my food,' said Lysander.

'You're wrong – it's our food,' said Agesilaus. 'I spotted it when Diokles asked me to check your sack.'

'Why didn't you tell Diokles?' said Lysander.

'If I hadn't kept quiet,' said Agesilaus, 'we'd have nothing at all. You're forgetting the Spartan way – cheating is fine, as long as you don't get caught.'

Agesilaus picked up the handful of peppermint leaves that lay strewn across the ground.

'Open your mouth,' he said. He grabbed Lysander's arm and twisted, kicking him hard in the kidney. 'Do as I tell you, half-breed!' Lysander struggled to breathe as the pain brought tears to his eyes. His arm was close to breaking. He opened his mouth in a cry of pain. Agesilaus stuffed the ruined peppermint leaves between Lysander's lips. 'Now, chew!'

Lysander's humiliation made him hate Agesilaus with a new passion. He forced himself to chew, grit and dirt grinding against his teeth. *I hate you!* Lysander silently swore at Agesilaus. The older boy watched to make sure that Lysander swallowed. Then with a nod of satisfaction, Agesilaus picked up the pouch of meat and tied it to his belt.

'I'm in charge of rations from now on,' said the bully. 'And don't you forget it.'

'Demaratos needed those leaves,' said Lysander. 'Why would you do that?'

Agesilaus laughed. 'Why not?' he smirked. 'I'm not here to look after you. My job is to make life hard for you two up here. If I walk back alone from the hills, the Elders will simply say you weren't strong enough. I've seen it happen before. For now, you'll have to collect those leaves again.'

'But there aren't any more,' Lysander protested, standing up.

'Down there.' Agesilaus gave Lysander a shove and

pointed to a ledge of rock that extended out from a headland about a hundred paces away. Lysander could see the green plants growing in the shelter of the cliff face.

'But how will I get down there?' asked Lysander.

Agesilaus laughed. 'Carefully! Now, hand over your sandals.'

'What?' said Lysander.

'You heard, slave,' said Agesilaus. 'They're a decent pair, and if you fall, I'll wear them myself – a memento of the great mothax, Lysander.'

'You're mad,' said Lysander. 'Those rocks are sharp as knives. I won't do it.'

Agesilaus' smile disappeared. 'If you don't, I'll throw you off myself. So, choose. A few scratches to your feet? Or your brains all over the rocks, picked at by crows.'

Agesilaus wasn't joking. Lysander bent down to unstrap his sandals, as Agesilaus watched closely. *I can do this*, he told himself. Agesilaus snatched the sandals from him.

'You can have them back at camp,' he said, walking back up the slope. 'If we see you again.'

Lysander approached the edge of the cliff. There was no obvious path down – the mountainside was almost vertical. The earth was broken and dusty, and a few sharp fragments of flint jutted from the hillside. Hundreds of feet below was a pine forest. Lysander felt dizzy just looking down there. He hated the idea of risking his life for Demaratos – a boy who had always treated him badly. But he couldn't forget Kassandra's words: *He's better than you think*. Plus, Lysander knew there was a part of him that didn't want to accept defeat. He wanted to show his compatriots that he could be brave – braver than either of them.

Lysander crouched low to the ground and turned, so that his back was facing the drop. Gripping a tree root, he lowered his right leg over the edge. His foot found a crevice. *One step at a time*, he told himself. *One step at a time*. Lysander lowered his other foot, taking most of his weight on his arms. Again, he managed to find a toehold. A shard of shingle sliced the tender flesh of his instep, and Lysander drew a sharp breath through his teeth. He could feel the air sting where the skin had been torn. But he had to go on. He lowered his feet further, and found a narrow ledge to balance on. Next he looked for a handhold. Leaning back to inspect the cliff face, his weight shifted. He realised his mistake immediately. There was a sound of sliding earth, and a sensation of weightlessness shot through him.

'No!' he cried out into the empty air. But it was too late.

Lysander was falling.

CHAPTER 6

Lysander slid down the rock face. His limbs scraped against the slope and the side of his face smashed into the hard-packed earth. Then his foot jarred on something, and his body jerked to one side. A blow crashed into his ribs, knocking the wind out of his lungs and rattling his teeth. A cry of pain escaped Lysander, but somehow he managed to find a handhold, grabbing hold of a slither of rock. He gasped for air while his legs dangled uselessly. Looking up, Lysander realised he had fallen about twenty feet.

'Help me!' he shouted, not caring that raw fear filled his voice. He heaved himself upwards, until his chest was level with the edge of the ledge, but he didn't have the strength in his arms to pull himself any higher. He sank back, defeated. 'Please! Somebody! Agesilaus!'

Come on! he told himself. An image flashed before his eyes: Agesilaus telling Sarpedon that he had died in the mountains, that he wasn't tough enough to prove himself. *You're not going to die here!* He took a deep breath and felt strength pulse into his arms and hands. He let out a cry through gritted teeth and pulled with all his might. A fraction at a time, he dragged his body upwards, until he got an elbow on to the ledge. It was enough. His other elbow followed as he hauled his body over the edge. He lay on his back, breathing hard, his heart knocking in his chest. His ribs were sore to touch, and he hoped he hadn't broken one of them. He put a hand to his cheek. The skin was grazed and already feeling bruised beneath. Other than that, only his fingertips, torn with trying to stop his descent, and his bloody knees and feet were evidence of how close death had been. Any further to the left, and the ledge would not have saved him. Above him, the eagle circled in the blue sky.

Lysander waited for his breathing to return to normal. Then he climbed stiffly to his feet and began to pick the peppermint leaves, one by one.

Lysander arrived back at the shelter to find Agesilaus sitting on a rock, chewing on a strip of dried meat.

'Your feet look sore,' he smirked, throwing Lysander's sandals at him. 'This is delicious, by the way.'

'Where's Demaratos?' asked Lysander, bending to fasten the sandals on to his bloody and filthy feet. He couldn't afford to use his water to wash them.

'I sent him to get firewood,' said Agesilaus. 'Here he comes now.'

Demaratos emerged from the trees near their

shelter, walking slowly with a handful of sticks clutched to his chest. They clattered to the ground when he saw Lysander.

'You treacherous swine!' he shouted. Demaratos came running at Lysander and tackled him in the middle with his shoulder, knocking him into the dirt. Then he pounded Lysander with tight fists, punches landing in Lysander's face and on his chest. Lysander lowered his elbow to protect his ribs and tried to ward off the blows to his face with his other arm.

'How dare you keep food from us!' shouted Demaratos. 'I'll tear you apart.'

Lysander bucked and managed to throw Demaratos off. His enemy didn't move. *He feels as weak as me*, thought Lysander.

'I was going to share it!' he shouted back. 'I was saving it for when we were desperate.'

'No, you weren't,' said Demaratos. 'You would have eaten it all. You only care about yourself!'

Lysander was too angry to say anything. Instead, he stood up slowly and fetched his sack from where it lay on the ground. He took out the peppermint leaves and threw them at Demaratos's feet.

'If I only cared about myself,' he shouted, 'why have I just risked my life to bring you these?' Demaratos looked at the leaves silently, and then at Lysander. 'Kassandra tried to tell me you weren't a vicious thug. But she was wrong.'

Demaratos's eyes fell to the ground.

60

'Chew them,' said Lysander in disgust. 'They'll settle your stomach. I'll go and get the rest of the firewood before the sun sets.'

'No, you won't,' said Agesilaus, swallowing a last mouthful of meat. 'It's Demaratos's task, and he's failed. There's not enough kindling there to warm an infant. We won't have a fire tonight.'

Lysander was past caring. He watched Demaratos scrabbling in the dirt, trying to rescue the crushed peppermint. His fury began to ease. Is this what it meant to be a Spartan? Turning on each other like animals, ready to fight like scavengers over scraps of food?

Lysander turned away from the boy on his knees and the older Spartan who laughed at them. He leant his head back and rubbed his knuckles into his sore eyes. Then he walked away, desperate for a few moments away from his mountain compatriots. *If I survive this*, he told himself, *I swear I'll never suffer such indignities again.* After everything he had endured as a Helot slave, this was worse. This was as bad as it got.

Morning brought back the pain. As soon as he opened his eyes Lysander felt nausea squirm in his stomach. He was going to be sick. He managed to scrabble a few paces away from where the other boys slept before retching. Nothing came but a gagging cough and a thin trickle of bitter yellow bile. After a few more convulsions, Lysander climbed to his feet and inspected his body in the pale light. A huge bruise, angry purple, spread under his chest on the left side. Part of it was spongy to the touch, definitely broken.

'Feeling hungry?' said Agesilaus behind him.

Demaratos, too, had stirred, and was looking at Agesilaus with a mixture of pleading and anger, as the older Spartan took out another piece of meat and held it under his nostrils.

'It smells very good,' he said, inhaling deeply. 'I want to give you your day's ration, but first you have to earn it. Show me what you've learnt in the barracks.'

'What do you mean?' asked Lysander.

'Well, you can start with some wrestling,' said Agesilaus. 'They say that Diokles isn't as tough as he once was. They say he's going soft on you youngsters.'

Demaratos and Lysander shared a panicked glance. Lysander knew how weak he was feeling – surely Demaratos was the same.

'You want us to wrestle each other?' said Demaratos quietly.

'That's right,' said the older boy. 'The winner gets this.' He held up the piece of meat. Lysander couldn't take his eyes from it. He would do anything for some food now, and even wondered if he could snatch it from Agesilaus' hands. He could run away, devour it and deal with the consequences later. But that was impossible. Agesilaus still looked strong and able – he was coping fine with the Ordeal.

'I'll do it,' said Demaratos, and flashed a look at Lysander.

Lysander knew he had no choice. 'Very well,' he said.

'Good,' said Agesilaus, smiling. 'The first to submit is the loser.'

Demaratos climbed slowly to his feet, never taking his gaze from Lysander. He was stood on slightly higher ground and already had an advantage. The look in his eyes reminded Lysander of a wild animal – focused and dangerous. Lysander longed to have the Fire of Ares hanging around his neck. He thought of the inscription written on the reverse. *The Fire of Ares shall inflame the righteous.* He needed that strength now. There was no way he could beat Demaratos – his bones felt fragile and his limbs sapped of energy.

Demaratos darted forward, and Lysander managed to skip out of his grasp, but an arm caught his rib, making his head spin. He held his hand to his side. A spark of annoyance flared. They circled, and now Lysander stood further up the slope.

'It's like watching two girls fighting,' said Agesilaus from his perch.

Demaratos came forward again, and this time he managed to get his hands around Lysander's waist. With a heave, Lysander felt his body lifted off the ground. He let out a cry, but there was nothing he could do. Demaratos threw him to the ground on his back, jarring his spine and knocking his breath out of him. The pain in his rib threatened to make him black out.

Demaratos was already sitting at his feet, and had Lysander's leg threaded between his own. He gripped Lysander's foot with his hand. Lysander realised he was trying to apply the lock that Diokles had taught them.

'I think this might be the end for you, Lysander,' came Agesilaus' voice.

Lysander had to do something – fast. He kicked at Demaratos's head, but he couldn't free himself. Demaratos found his grip and tightened the lock. Pain shot through Lysander's knee and ankle as Demaratos twisted his foot. There was only one chance left . . . With his free leg, Lysander aimed a kick at Demaratos's shoulder – the one he'd dislocated on the night of the Festival Games. His heel crunched home.

'Helot dog!' Demaratos cried. Lysander felt his grip loosen. It was just enough. He pulled the foot free and aimed another kick, this time at Demaratos's face. It connected with his chin. Demaratos's jaw gave a crunching sound and he collapsed backwards. He was unconscious. Lysander stood over him. Blood trickled from Demaratos's mouth.

What have I done? thought Lysander.

A slow clapping noise came from behind. Agesilaus was climbing down from his rock.

'I'm impressed, Lysander,' he said. 'You exploited Demaratos's weakness. That sort of determination and cunning will stand you in good stead on the battlefield. My tutor used to tell me: all is not lost until the blood runs cold in a Spartan's veins.' He tossed a piece of the dried meat at Lysander's feet. Lysander didn't care about the dust. He sank to his knees and grabbed the pork, stuffing it into his mouth. The salty tang tasted delicious – Lysander had never known something could taste so good. At first, he swallowed without chewing, but the meat would not last long and he knew he would soon be hungry again. He forced himself to savour the last precious bites.

Agesilaus bent over Demaratos and gave him a sharp slap to the side of the head. The sound echoed away across the hills. Demaratos groaned and opened his eyes groggily. When he saw Lysander with the food, the disappointment was written in his eyes. Lysander swallowed, and his throat burned. He felt his face flush with shame.

'Here,' he said, tearing off a piece of meat and holding it out to Demaratos. 'Take this.'

Demaratos stared in disbelief at the gift, but then snatched at the meat as though worried that Lysander might take back the offer.

'Thank you,' he said hesitantly. The words clearly didn't come easily to him. Agesilaus glared at the two of them.

'I was wrong about you, Lysander. You're no Spartan, after all. Your heart is soft.' He turned away in disgust, but Demaratos shared a secret smile with Lysander and Lysander found himself smiling back. He reached out a hand and helped Demaratos to his feet. For the first time since entering the barracks, Lysander and

Demaratos stood eye-to-eye and neither of them turned away.

'I may have a soft heart,' Lysander muttered as he gazed after the older boy, 'but I have the sense to spy an enemy.'

'Me too,' said Demaratos, flicking a glance at Agesilaus. 'We would do well to watch each other's backs.'

Lysander hesitated, then nodded. Demaratos was right. The two of them would survive better as friends. They started to follow Agesilaus up the hill. Lysander's mind was reeling. *Can I trust this boy?* he wondered. Lysander had no choice; he had to. But more than that – something had changed. Now, he wanted to.

As they caught up with Agesilaus he turned and stopped them in their tracks. His lip curled in a sneer as he gazed at Lysander.

'So, boy, are you ready for your latest challenge?'

'I'm ready,' he said. 'What is it?'

Agesilaus pointed further up the mountain, where the snow-crested slopes were brushed by thick clouds.

'Up there,' he said.

Lysander followed Agesilaus up the steep mountain path. They'd left Demaratos behind to find more firewood for the camp. There wasn't much greenery up here – just grey rocks. Among the sparse fir trees, Lysander saw an eagle again, soaring majestically overhead.

As they climbed higher, Lysander found himself

short of breath. He felt dizzy and realised that the thin mountain air combined with an empty stomach were almost enough to make him faint. He'd never felt so weak. He found a fallen branch, crooked, but sturdy enough, and used it as a walking stick. He felt like one of the old Helots who wandered around the settlements, begging for food.

Agesilaus looked round to make sure Lysander was keeping up.

'Pathetic,' he said, when he saw Lysander heaving himself up the mountainside, leaning heavily on his stick. Lysander didn't have the breath to reply. Agesilaus turned and continued to stride ahead. Nothing seemed to get to the older boy; it was obvious his harsh training had made him fiercely capable.

They reached the snowline as the light began to fade. What started as a patch of snow here and there, soon gave way to larger swathes of ice. Wisps of cloud drifted across their path, enveloping them in ghostly mist. Agesilaus paused to take a drink from his flask. Watching him, Lysander realised he'd left his sack at camp. He looked at the snow. Just a mouthful would quench his thirst. He scooped some up.

'Don't be a fool!' said Agesilaus. 'Has Diokles taught you nothing? Eating snow will chill your body more. It's a quick route to death.'

Lysander dropped the snow, and licked the moisture from his hand. He noticed how quickly the sweat from the climb cooled on his body. Looking back, he couldn't even spot the path on which they had ascended, but a thin line of smoke told him where Demaratos was sheltering far below. The brow of the hill hid Sparta and the outlying settlements from view. The mist closed in again, and pricks of ice landed on Lysander's face. The first flakes of snow were falling.

'Do we have to go much further?' he asked. They'd be walking back in the dark.

The older boy looked up the slope.

'Not far now,' he replied, and pressed on.

Lysander followed, dread filling his heart.

The snow grew deeper. Everything was white now, and a blizzard whipped around their bodies. All Lysander's faint warmth was long gone. One side of his face was completely numb. The blood from his injured feet had frozen in the intense cold. Now the soles of his feet were stuck to the inside of his sandals; every step was like tearing open a fresh scab. Agesilaus stopped a few paces ahead, and the outline of his body blurred in and out as the snow thickened and flurried. Lysander eventually drew level with him.

'Was that the challenge?' he asked. He was leaning heavily on his stick now.

Agesilaus turned to Lysander, looking him up and down. His eyebrows and hair were dusted with snow.

'Time to head back,' he said.

Lysander's heart lifted. Thank the Gods it was over. Agesilaus was already starting to make his way back down the mountain, and Lysander hobbled after him.

Agesilaus turned. 'Where are you going?'

'You said it was time to head back,' said Lysander.

Agesilaus put a hand on Lysander's chest, and then gave a fierce shove. There was no time for Lysander to react. He lost his balance, and fell back into the snow.

'I said it was time for me to go back,' he said. 'Your trial has only just begun. If you descend back from this mountain before dawn, I swear by Zeus himself that I'll kill you with my own hands.'

Lysander watched Agesilaus' face for signs that he was joking.

'Are you mad? No one could survive up here!'

But Agesilaus had already turned away and was beginning his descent. His laughter was whipped away by the howling wind.

Agesilaus had lost his mind! Lysander knew for sure he would freeze to death up here. The snow was already seeping through his tunic. He clambered to his feet. Darkness would soon be upon the slopes and any warmth from the sun would be lost.

Lysander looked frantically about – there must be a way to get through this. He couldn't remember ever being this cold before. He looked at his hands, the fingers purple and stiff, willing them to move. He could feel panic rising up through him.

'Stay calm,' he said out loud. 'Don't give in.'

He peered up through the flurries of snow to the craggy mountain tops. Could there be some shelter up

69

there, a spot out of the wind and snow? There was only one way to find out.

Lysander pulled his frozen right foot from the snow and took a slow, clumsy step. Then another, placing his left foot in front of his right.

Slowly, Lysander began to climb.

CHAPTER 7

Lysander stumbled blindly through the snow. He knew he was losing his battle against the cold. Ice was beginning to set in his hair. The hills that had always looked so beautiful from the settlement now felt treacherous. Deep shivers racked his body. Every bone ached and his broken rib sang with pain. Tears came to his eyes. They were warm at first, but cooled quickly to ice.

'You have to keep going!' he yelled into the wind and snow.

The snow continued to swirl around him; everything was white. Lysander twisted around, looking for any vantage point, but there was nothing. He couldn't feel his feet or his ankles any more. And he realised he could no longer see the mountain peaks. Lysander had lost his bearings. It was hopeless. He had to get off the mountain – now. Agesilaus need never know. *If I stay up here*, he thought, *I'm as good as dead*.

He started walking, dragging his freezing feet through the snow. It didn't feel as though he were losing height, but he didn't think he was gaining it either. He decided he must be skirting the edge of the hill. Lysander remembered the cliffs from earlier. What if he was walking straight towards the edge? He wouldn't even see it coming. There would be a stomach-churning drop, before his body was smashed on the rocks below. *A horrible way to die.*

Lysander trudged a few more paces, sinking up to his knees in the deep drifts, but he knew he was wandering aimlessly. He could be anywhere. He could feel the ice closing around his heart. His hands may as well have been made of wood.

'Help!' he shouted. Lysander's lips were numb and the words came out slurred. 'Help me!' he yelled again. There was no reply. The snow absorbed the sound, muffling his voice like a pillow over a face. He took another step forward. The snow collapsed, its white surface giving way with a soft sigh. Before Lysander could reach out to stop himself, he'd fallen up to his middle in the snowdrift. Trapped! Snow and ice pressed up against him on all sides. But as Lysander struggled to climb out, he realised that, if anything, the packed snow was warmer than the icy wind. A vague memory stirred: sitting by the fire with his mother as she told her stories. What was it she had told him about travellers lost in the mountains?

Lysander found that even his mind was slowing down now. His eyelids drooped and he felt sleepy. It seemed to take longer between telling his body to

72

move and the movement itself. He shook his head to clear his thoughts. He tried to remember his mother's face, but his brain refused to work.

What had his mother said? They used to survive by digging holes, chambers in the fallen snow. Anything to keep their bodies sheltered from the wind. *They buried themselves alive?* That couldn't be right, surely. His eyes drooped shut. He told himself to wake up and slowly they opened again.

The cold didn't seem to matter so much any more, though he was aware of his body shivering and his teeth chattering uncontrollably. If he could only sleep, everything would be fine. He shook his head. *No!* he told himself. *You have to stay awake.* He tried to call out for help again, but his voice came out even more weakly this time. His mother's words echoed through his head.

Bury yourself alive. It meant something.

Bury yourself.

Lysander scooped snow towards him using his clawed hands. He packed the snow against his torso, working as quickly as his frozen limbs would allow. The wind whistled around him, like some demented flute.

'Come on,' he said out loud. 'Don't give up.' He let his body rest against the bank of snow he'd built up around him. With his last reserves of strength he dragged more piles of snow around his head, leaving a small gap to breathe. The whistling wind melted away as the sides of his head were submerged. Nothing now. The snow was damp next to his skin, but his shivering was already subsiding. Through the small hole, he watched fat flakes of snow falling through the immense silence, adding to the heavy blanket of ice.

Lysander concentrated on slowing his breathing. Could the shallow grave be working? He didn't dare move, for fear of disturbing the rest of the snowdrift and bringing it down over his head. He did manage to shift his arm though, so that his palm rested over his chest. The place where the Fire of Ares had always been. Even without the pendant itself, Lysander felt its power. He clutched the imaginary red jewel. *You'll make it*, he told himself. *You'll get through the night.*

Looking up, he saw that the clouds were thinning, revealing patches of night sky. Stars twinkled. Lysander was too weak to move, and his eyes blurred in and out of focus as his eyelids became heavy. He had no way of knowing whether it was sleep or death that was drawing him near.

But something strange was happening in the sky. A collection of stars directly above seemed to move in the firmament, vibrating in time with his heartbeat, becoming brighter than the rest. Was it a trick of his mind? He watched as the glowing stars appeared to drift towards one another. They coalesced into a ring, which melted to an oval. Lysander thought he must be dreaming, but the constellation became a face. He wasn't afraid. He knew who this was.

'Father,' said Lysander through cracked lips. Though he had never seen his father Thorakis, Lysander felt a flash of recognition. 'Father, help me,' he whispered.

The face shimmered and smiled reassuringly.

Warmth suffused Lysander's body, as though his blood had turned molten. The snow was no longer his enemy – it caressed him. The blood once again pulsed through his veins. His father was watching over him.

Lysander let his eyelids close. Then he fell into the embrace of Hypnos, God of Sleep.

Lysander was woken by warm light, orange behind his eyelids. He opened his eyes. Above him glowed an iridescent blue sky. Damp snow crushed against his lips. He'd survived! Elation turned to panic when Lysander realised he was trapped – he couldn't move. Under the snow, his arms felt heavy, like they were made of iron. Lysander strained with his whole body under the drift, his heart pounding. The snow shifted, but only a little, and he had to sink back defeated. Patiently, he told his fingertips to move. They wriggled weakly in the snow. Lysander was breathing hard with the exertion, but he wouldn't be beaten. With regular movement, the snow around his hand began to melt. A dull, but satisfying ache seeped into his limbs, and he managed to work his hand from under the snow. He was nearly there, and began to shovel the layer of snow away from around his body. Pulling his torso free, he scrambled to his feet, laughing for joy.

'I'm alive!' he shouted. 'I'm alive!' His voice echoed in the still morning air.

Lysander stood and shook the loose snow from his clothes, just as the sun winked over the horizon, and began to warm his stiff and aching limbs. The sky was bursting with light, and everything was peaceful, covered in a pristine layer. He looked around him to try to find his bearings. The path, if there was one, was invisible. But neither could he see the cliff edge he'd been so worried about. Below, trees were weighed down with snow. He couldn't wait to climb down. What would Demaratos say when he saw him again? Would Agesilaus be angry? Lysander didn't care. His laughter echoed off the mountainside.

He began to crunch down the slope, the crisp new snow creaking under each footstep. Gradually the blood flowed back into his feet. A screech from above made him turn to the sky. A solitary eagle hung in the air, spreading its wings. Lysander had never been so close to the Gods. The eagle tilted and wheeled away, disappearing from view around the mountain's shoulder.

Lysander ran, half stumbling down the mountainside. As he entered the treeline, he grabbed low branches to slow his descent. Snow showered down on him but now Lysander no longer cared.

The eagle had reappeared, circling overhead as though guiding him down from the slopes.

'Are you following me?' Lysander shouted jubilantly.

As the snow became sparser on the ground, the familiar path came once again into view. Picking his way among the trees and rocks, his strength sapped away again. His legs were weak, and he struggled to keep moving. But the exhilaration of his survival gave his tired limbs the extra push they needed.

Agesilaus would not be expecting to see him again, of that he was sure. Whether the delirious vision of his father was real or not, Lysander knew that something had given him the will to make it through the night. Lysander paused and craned his neck back to look up at the clear blue sky, scored with the faintest wisps of cloud. The eagle circled the air. Then, with a cry of farewell, the huge bird caught an eddy of air that carried him back up the mountain. Lysander raised his hands to shield his eyes against the morning sun and watched the bird's departure. His mountain friend had gone. But as Lysander turned back towards camp, he didn't feel alone.

'I faced death and I survived,' Lysander said to himself. Then he threw his arms wide to embrace the new day. 'I made it!' he cried.

CHAPTER 8

As Lysander rounded the edge of the camp, Agesilaus was sharpening the end of a makeshift spear with a piece of flint. A twig snapped under Lysander's foot and Agesilaus leapt to his feet, brandishing the weapon, his lips parted in surprise.

'Who's there?' he shouted. Lysander paused and waited while Agesilaus registered that the attacker was the boy he'd left to his death in the mountains. He clenched his mouth closed and the hard look returned to his green eyes.

'You're back,' he said, lowering the spear. His tone held the hint of interrogation.

'I slept in a shallow grave,' said Lysander.

Demaratos wandered out of the cave. He rushed forward and clapped Lysander on the back.

'You made it!' he said. 'Agesilaus said you were sure to die!'

'Well, I didn't,' said Lysander, fixing the older boy with a stare.

'I trust you spent a snug night?' Agesilaus sneered.

'Yes,' replied Lysander. 'It was hard to build a shelter in the snow, but I did it.'

'Maybe you're not as useless as your tutor said. Anyway, you're back in time to see Demaratos complete his trial,' said Agesilaus. 'There's a herd of goats living further down the hill. I've seen their droppings. Demaratos is going to catch us some breakfast, using his bare hands.'

'No problem,' said Demaratos, straightening his shoulders. 'How hard can it be?'

Lysander ducked into their open cave to retrieve his sack. He pulled his water flask out and took a deep swig of water. But on the first mouthful he gagged, spitting on the ground.

'It's salt water!' cried Lysander, wiping the strings of saliva from his mouth. It was a bitter blow after his night of torture.

Demaratos unstoppered his own flask and tasted the water, then spat it out with disgust.

'A little gift from Diokles,' laughed Agesilaus. 'He didn't want to make the Ordeal too easy. Come on, the goats will still be dozy.'

Lysander and Demaratos shared a glance of misery. But what was the point in attacking Agesilaus? They couldn't bring him down and besides – this is what they'd been sent into the mountains for. To be tested, beyond anything they had ever suffered before.

The three of them set off down the slope, Agesilaus

carrying his spear, and Lysander more hungry and thirsty than ever. He could almost taste the roasted goat meat. They entered a thicket of trees in single file. Lysander saw the piles of round droppings. They were still fresh. Agesilaus suddenly pulled up.

'I can't see any . . .' started Demaratos, but Agesilaus raised a finger to his lips.

Ahead, Lysander could hear a rustling. Something was making its way towards them along the forest floor. Lysander felt the hairs at the back of his neck stand up, and his heart knocked in his chest.

'Follow me!' hissed Agesilaus. Lysander dropped into a crouch and placed his feet carefully among the fallen branches and pine cones. The three of them moved forward. They came to a gloomy clearing, and hid behind a clump of holly bushes. At first, Lysander couldn't see anything. But as he watched, a movement came from the far side of the open space. A branch had fallen there and something was behind it, rummaging for food.

Agesilaus pointed his spear at Demaratos, then into the clearing.

'It's yours!' he whispered.

Demaratos gave a nod and broke cover, moving stealthily around the outside of the clearing, edging closer to the goat. Lysander looked on intently. *Don't let us down*, he willed. If they didn't get a good meal soon, they were as good as dead. The rustling stopped. *Now!* urged Lysander. *Before it escapes.*

There was a fierce grunt, and Demaratos let out a shout of alarm. A squat black-haired creature burst from the leaves – a wild boar! Short yellow horns protruded from either side of its lower jaw, and red eyes glowed fiercely. The boar shot across the ground towards Demaratos. It bowled into his legs and knocked him to the floor. It quickly skidded in a half circle and charged again. In seconds it was on top of Demaratos, squealing and grunting. Lysander saw the flash of teeth and pink gums. Demaratos's desperate shouts made Lysander shudder.

'Help me!' yelled Demaratos. 'Please, help.'

Lysander looked towards Agesilaus. The older Spartan was leaning on his spear and grinning.

'Do something!' shouted Lysander.

Demaratos managed to push the beast off of him, and started to scramble away, but the boar was relentless. Its teeth clamped around Demaratos's leg, and he screamed in pain, before falling to the ground. Lysander knew how dangerous wild boars could be – he remembered the horribly scarred face of Solon. If he didn't help Demaratos now, he might be killed. Lysander ran at Agesilaus, and grabbed the spear that he was holding loosely.

'Hey, stop!' shouted the Spartan.

Lysander ignored him. He charged towards the boar and took aim, ramming the spear into the creature's side. It gave a yelp and immediately withdrew, the spear sticking out of his flesh. The shaft of the spear was torn

81

from Lysander's hands as the boar retreated. It turned twice on the spot, reaching with its mouth to where the shaft hung from its muscular flank, then careered off into the bushes.

Demaratos staggered to his feet. His hands were bloodied where he had fended off the boar's teeth, and his tunic was badly torn. Thick blood coursed down his leg where the animal had sunk its jaws into his flesh. A loose flap of skin was hanging off. Demaratos's face was pale with fear. He almost fell again, but Lysander steadied him.

'I failed,' he said, not meeting Lysander's eyes.

'At least you're still alive,' Lysander reassured him.

'Thanks to you,' said Demaratos. 'You saved my life.'

'Yes, and he lost my spear, and the boar!' shouted Agesilaus. He stepped out of the clearing. 'Don't you ever dare take my weapon again.'

Further down the slope, they trudged out of the bottom end of the forest on to a plateau. The vista took Lysander's breath away. He could see Sparta in the distance: the five villages and the surrounding settlements where the Helots scraped together a living. Up here in the mountains, without their red cloaks and weapons, it didn't matter whether Lysander was Spartan or Helot. The elements had no respect for either. Lysander was caked with dirt, and covered with scratches. His tunic was torn, and he felt hunger like a knot of pain. Without food and water, everyone was equal. It didn't matter if you were born a noble or a slave — it was how you behaved that counted. The Fire of Ares had taught him that.

Demaratos tripped on the path and fell to his knees. He began to retch. Lysander knelt beside him and placed a comforting hand on his back.

'Leave him,' said Agesilaus. 'He's slowing us down.'

Lysander stared at his companions. Both Agesilaus and Demaratos looked awful, with hollow cheeks and dark circles under their eyes. He knew that he looked the same. It was impossible to ignore the hunger that gnawed at his insides.

'We can't carry on like this,' said Lysander. 'If we don't find food soon, we'll all starve.'

'And what do you propose to do about that, Lysander?' asked Agesilaus.

Lysander gazed down to where the Helot settlement, the site of his old house, sprawled across the land beneath the hills. He thought about the meals of stewed lentils and stale bread that he used to share with his mother. His mouth watered at the memory. Agesilaus came to stand beside him and looked down at the settlement.

'A true Spartan would take food from one of those houses,' he said in Lysander's ear. 'I bet they have bread, cheese and maybe even some meat.'

'I can't steal from a Helot — they have next to nothing as it is.' Lysander said. But he could feel the stain of doubt spreading through his heart. Could he?

He and his companions were close to starvation.

'Can't, or won't?' said Agesilaus, and spat on the ground. 'You're a Spartan now, remember. The Helot slaves owe us everything in their possession. Do you think you'd make a good thief?'

Lysander's stomach answered for him, letting out a loud grumble.

'That's what I thought,' said Agesilaus.

'Please, Lysander,' said Demaratos. He was still limping from where the boar had attacked him. He had torn off a strip of his tunic and tied it over the wound. 'You don't have to steal a lot. Just enough for the three of us.'

Lysander looked again at the settlement. Demaratos was right. The Helots were desperate people, but right now, who had the biggest need?

'I'll do it,' Lysander said. He started to walk in the direction of the settlement. Agesilaus and Demaratos trailed after him. If this is what it took in order to eat, Lysander could steal. *Just don't ask me to be proud of myself*, he thought. He remembered the vision that he'd had in the mountains. Would his father be proud of him now? Lysander doubted it.

By late morning they reached the edge of the settlement. From a low escarpment, Lysander surveyed the territory. There were few people about; they would mostly be in the fields. A group of women were watching over several young children, who played in a

84

small meadow beside the outer houses. An elderly man cleaned vegetables in a bucket of dirty water. Lysander remembered the last time he was at the settlement – the night of the flogging. Timeon's ragged back where the whip fell. His groans of agony. Diokles laughing at each stroke. He pushed the memories away.

'You must not be seen,' said Agesilaus. 'A Spartan steals, but is never caught.'

'Wait here,' Lysander replied. 'I'll be back soon.' He started to climb down, away from his companions.

'Crawl, dog,' Agesilaus hissed from behind him. Lysander lowered himself on to his belly and slithered along the ground, watchful all the time. He was filled with shame.

As he came nearer to the houses, the smells of morning cooking found their way to him. There was no way Lysander was going back empty-handed. He had reached a small hovel. Edging along the wall, Lysander looked down one of the pathways that threaded between the huts. Two old women were washing clothes out in the street, wringing the water into the open sewers, talking in low voices. He darted behind them into another alley. Lysander suddenly recognised where he was. The beam above the low doorway of the house ahead was painted with the symbol of horns overflowing with grain – a charm to bring prosperity from the fields. It was a door he had seen hundreds of times before. Timeon's house. He remembered the last time he saw his friend – the raw welts across his back – and felt a stab of anguish. He steadied himself against the wall, then broke cover. Keeping hidden no longer seemed important. As he stumbled into the street, the noises of the settlement faded out of his consciousness. The door beckoned him and he found his steps drawn towards the hut. *Perhaps Timeon is in there now*, he thought.

Lysander approached the door and stepped under the low threshold. For the first time in days, his hunger lifted and he felt calm. He could almost have travelled back in time, to before the days he learnt about the Fire of Ares' significance. He might have been calling on his friend before they headed out to the fields. But so much had changed, and couldn't be changed back.

The dark hut was bigger than the single room he used to share with his mother, because both Timeon's parents were alive, and he had a younger sister, Sophia. By any standards, though, it was basic, with the hearth at one end, and a low bench in front of it. The two bedrooms were separated by a curtain and were reached by passing under a crude wooden arch. Lysander noticed a bag of oats by the far wall and a couple of onions. There were several pots also, probably containing honey or olives. Two loaves of bread were wrapped in cloth, and a string of garlic hung from a peg. Hunger knotted his insides. A fragrant scent of wild flowers filled the air.

'Timeon?' he whispered. There was no answer. Lysander crept inside the bedroom, and stopped. The smell was stronger here. Two candles flickered at the foot of a raised trestle table, and oil burned in a bowl. On the table was a shrouded object. From the way the cotton sheet dipped and folded around the contours, Lysander knew it was a body.

Lysander approached the table and took hold of a corner of the sheet.

'Traitor,' said a voice behind him. Lysander spun around, his heart racing. Under the arch stood Timeon's mother.

'Hecuba?' he said.

'How dare you come into my house, after what you did?' she seethed, her whole body trembling. Goose pimples prickled and tightened Lysander's skin. Who was under the shroud? Why would Timeon's mother call him a traitor? The truth closed in around Lysander like a swarm of rats, forcing their way over the threshold of his consciousness. Turning his back on Timeon's mother, he pulled back the shroud. The eyes that were once so full of life were closed, and the skin pale, almost waxy. No smile lit up that face. It was Timeon.

CHAPTER 9

Lysander's stomach reeled and he dropped to his knees beside the table. Timeon, his best friend since he could crawl, was dead. He had only fourteen summers behind him.

Lysander remembered Timeon's eyes, reflected in the water of the trough. The weight of the whip in Lysander's hand.

Lysander turned towards Hecuba, who was standing with her arms over her chest. He scrabbled across the floor and gripped the hem of her dress.

'Please,' he uttered. 'Please forgive me. I was forced to do it. Timeon . . . he was made to as well. I didn't mean to hurt him so badly. How can he have died? It was the Spartans . . .'

'You are a Spartan now,' snapped Hecuba.

Lysander raised his head and looked into her eyes. Her bloodless lips were pressed tightly together.

'No,' said Lysander. 'You don't understand. Timeon was my friend. I'm still a Helot. I'm only . . .'

'Would a Helot do this?' interrupted Timeon's mother, tearing Lysander's hands from the hem of her clothes and marching towards the shroud. She pulled it roughly aside to reveal Timeon's upper body, almost luminescent in the gloom.

Lysander saw it straight away. Around three ribs down, almost hidden by Timeon's arm, there was a messy gash in his torso, a wide tear in the skin. He climbed to his feet and moved closer. Hecuba didn't speak and moved aside. Lysander inspected the ragged edges of the wound. A sharp object had made it, a spear-tip perhaps, or a sword. Lysander knew from his sword lessons at the barracks where to stab in order to kill. This was a killing strike for sure. Whatever the weapon, it must have penetrated Timeon's lung, maybe going even as far as his heart. Hecuba's face was furrowed with anger.

'You don't think I did it?' Lysander said quietly.

'Why not, Lysander?' she snapped back. 'You do their bidding like the rest. Like a puppet. They say "Kill" and you obey. Who's to say that you wouldn't kill a friend? Who's to say you didn't kill my boy?'

Her face dissolved in grief. She repeated 'my boy' over and over until her voice was lost in weeping. She beat her chest with small, bony fists.

'Stop!' said Lysander. 'You'll hurt yourself.'

She didn't seem to hear him. Lysander stepped towards her, putting his arms around her. She writhed, trying to push him away – then gave in to his embrace.

She was smaller than he remembered and her tears soaked through the shoulder of his tunic. Her body shook with sobs. Lysander realised he too was crying. Hot tears of anger and grief. He'd never see his friend smile again. From outside, the noise of a Helot man singing tunelessly penetrated the walls. It was an old harvester's song, about gathering the golden crops.

As their weeping subsided, he led Hecuba over to a seat in the main room.

'I should never have let Timeon go to the barracks with you. The idea of him surrounded by Spartans terrified me. But he liked it, you see. He liked being with you.'

'I know,' said Lysander. 'Without Timeon to look after me, I wouldn't have survived the first months.' He remembered the times his friend had tended to his wounds, or convinced him that he still had strength to continue. Among all the other students, even Orpheus and Leonidas, Timeon had been Lysander's dearest and most loyal friend. 'You must know I could never kill him.' He paused. 'That night, the whippings, it was madness. But Timeon knew neither of us had any choice. They would have killed him if I hadn't obeyed them. They would have killed us both.'

'But they killed him anyway,' said Timeon's mother angrily. 'After we brought him inside and dressed his wounds, we all slept again. But by dawn, Timeon was dead. Some Spartan must have crept in at night and slaughtered him.' The bitter edge had returned to her voice. 'They take everything from us. Our land, our dignity . . . even our children. My child! My poor child! I should have been punished, not my boy.'

She suddenly stood and walked towards the fire glowing in the grate, thrusting her hand towards the orange embers.

'No!' said Lysander, darting after her. He was too late, she was already there. But she didn't put her hand in the flames. Instead, Hecuba reached up the narrow chimney and quickly pulled out an object from between soot-stained bricks. Timeon's mother came forward with the object in her hand, and placed it carefully in Lysander's palm. It was something wrapped in tattered leather.

'What is it?' asked Lysander, staring into Hecuba's sunken eyes.

'See for yourself,' she replied.

Lysander pulled the covering aside to reveal a beautifully carved piece of ash wood a little smaller than his hand. He rubbed his thumb tenderly across the grooves in the wood. He remembered when Timeon used to take out this slab of wood, and carefully carve with a sharp piece of flint. The shapes meant nothing; they meant everything as well. Timeon shone from every detail of the polished carving. It was the sort of trinket that the Spartans would confiscate if they ever discovered it.

'He would have wanted you to have this,' said Hecuba.

'It's all you have to remember him by,' protested Lysander.

'That's not true,' said Timeon's mother, closing his fingers over the carving. 'I have many things to remember my son by. Most of them are in here.' She tapped her chest above her heart. Her eyes wandered down Lysander, taking in his ravaged appearance. 'Is there anything I can give you? You aren't looking well.'

Lysander couldn't stop himself from glancing at the meagre supplies of food.

'I'm very hungry,' he said. 'We are living in the mountains as a test of strength. Food is scarce . . .'

Hecuba pointed to the supplies near the door.

'Take what you need, Lysander. Take all of it. I don't want to see a second boy die. The other Helots have been generous after Timeon's death. We will not go short.'

Lysander hurried over and grabbed one of the onions, sinking his teeth through the dirty skin and into the bitter flesh. It tasted wonderful. He chewed, skin and all, letting the juices fill his mouth. Then he remembered his dignity.

'I'm sorry,' he said. 'I haven't eaten for days.'

'I can see that,' said Hecuba. 'Fill your flask with water outside as well.'

Lysander put two of the pots, along with the garlic and a loaf of bread in his sack.

'Before you leave,' said Hecuba, coming towards him, 'say a final farewell to my son. He would appreciate it.' Lysander looked into her eyes, the rims swollen and red. For an instant, he saw his own mother. He nodded and shouldered the sack, before stepping back into the room where Timeon lay.

Lysander pulled the shroud back up to his friend's neck, and touched the skin on Timeon's forehead. It was cold and smooth, like marble. His friend had deserved so much more. It seemed impossible that his life could be extinguished.

'If you can hear me, Timeon,' whispered Lysander. 'I promise that I'll never forget you. You'll always be my friend.'

He laid the shroud over Timeon's blank face, and walked back into the main room. Hecuba was weeping quietly once again, and Lysander placed a hand against her arm. But there was nothing he could do for Timeon's mother now. Nothing could bring Timeon back.

Lysander suddenly realised how long he had been gone. He didn't want Agesilaus or Demaratos descending into the settlement. Who knew what havoc they would cause in their desperation for food?

'I must go,' he said quietly. 'Please, give my love to Sophia.'

He made his way towards the door. After a glance into the alley, he quickly stepped out.

The light was crisp and bright as Lysander weaved between the houses. The food at his side would save his life, but the death of his friend would never leave him.

Having filled the water flask at the trough, he finished the onion and climbed to where Agesilaus and Demaratos were waiting. He opened the sack and showed them the food. Their eyes widened.

'How did you get all that?' asked Agesilaus, with suspicion in his eyes.

'I stole it, of course,' said Lysander.

'Let's get back to the shelter before we eat,' said Agesilaus. 'We'll need a fire. I'll dish out rations.'

Together, the three of them moved quickly back up the hillside. The thought of food in his belly gave Lysander strength.

'We'll eat well tonight,' said Demaratos, smiling at Lysander.

'We will,' said Agesilaus, barely looking over his shoulder at them. 'We'll have a feast.'

Lysander watched Agesilaus' back as the older boy strode up the hill. He didn't spare a glance for the Helot settlement they left behind. Lysander's trip had served its purpose – the boys had food. Why should any of them care about the slaves in the village? But Lysander did care. In the mountains, Lysander had been at death's door. Now he knew that his friend, Timeon, had already walked through it.

CHAPTER 10

Lysander knocked the flint against the stone. Nothing.

'You couldn't light a fire if Prometheus himself gave you a flaming torch,' said Agesilaus.

Lysander brought the flint on to the stone again.

'Come on!' said Demaratos. 'I'm starving!'

Lysander repeated the action. This time a spark flew off the stone into the moss he'd shredded. A tiny orange glow caught in the centre. Cupping his hands around the tinder, Lysander blew into the hollow. He watched a thin trickle of smoke rise through the gaps between his fingers, then placed the smouldering moss gently beneath the firewood, and bent to blow more air into the base of the structure. A small crackle became louder as the kindling caught, and soon Lysander could see tongues of flames flickering between the frame of twigs.

'I did it!' he exclaimed.

Agesilaus grunted as Demaratos mixed oats and water in a badly chipped pot he'd found on the slope above the Helot settlement. Agesilaus hung it from a wooden A-frame over the licking flames. While they waited for the porridge to come to the boil, they ate some of the olives and roasted the garlic by the fireside.

Lysander rescued the garlic bulb as it began to char. He squeezed a large clove between finger and thumb, popping it from its skin. As his teeth sank into it, the flavour burst across his tongue. He closed his eyes and chewed. Lysander didn't think he'd ever tasted anything so good.

Once the porridge was cooked, they scooped in the honey and ate the mixture with their hands. Demaratos greedily plunged his fingers into the pot and licked his fingers. But after a few mouthfuls the sticky sweetness of the porridge was too much for Lysander.

'Not hungry?' said Agesilaus through a mouthful of oats.

Lysander shook his head. He thought back to his friend's body lying cold and still in his home. The other two finished their meals, wiping the pot clean using leaves plucked from the trees. Demaratos used a little of the water to clean his leg wound, and rubbed ash from the fire over it as an antiseptic.

'We'll move on tomorrow,' said Agesilaus. 'We need to find some more water, and there are streams to the south. Plus, I have another test for you both.'

Lysander didn't like the sound of it, but knew there was nothing he could do but wait until tomorrow.

'For now,' said their guide, 'let's get some sleep. The

firewood has almost run out.'

As Lysander lay down on the ground, Demaratos approached him, limping slightly.

'I wanted to say thank you,' he said, not managing to meet Lysander's eyes. 'For getting that food. I wouldn't have lasted much longer.'

'I needed it too,' replied Lysander. 'We must help each other up here,' he whispered.

Demaratos nodded and a smile flickered at the corners of his mouth.

Lysander listened while his two companions dropped quickly into an exhausted sleep, their breathing slowing. Demaratos wasn't so bad when there weren't others to show off to.

Through the leaves that covered the shelter, Lysander gazed up at the twinkling stars. His mother always used to say that the stars were the eyes of the dead, vigilant even in the darkness. After seeing the image of his father the night before, Lysander wondered if she was right. Was his mother also looking down from the heavens? Was she proud of Lysander, or ashamed? And how would his father Thorakis feel, following his behaviour in the Ordeal?

A chilling thought penetrated his mind: perhaps Timeon was watching too. He had understood Lysander's heart better than anyone. He had stood by him through the agoge, giving him the strength to carry on. But would he recognise Lysander's heart now?

The thought sent him into an uneasy sleep.

＊　＊　＊

Lysander slept through until dawn. When he woke, Agesilaus was already standing by the entrance of the shelter and looking south.

'I wondered when you two would bother to wake,' he said. 'We have a long day ahead. First of all, some marching practice.'

They finished the bread and honey from the night before. Then they set off, following the contours of the hill, as the sun rose to the east. For the first time, the mountains held no terror for him. With food in his belly, Lysander felt hopeful. They had survived four full days living on nothing but their instincts and guile. He was already imagining getting back to the barracks, seeing Orpheus and Leonidas once again. He wondered what they were doing now.

The only animals they saw were the occasional rabbit, a fluffy tail disappearing down a hole, and the red squirrels that hopped between the branches of the trees. Birds, startled at their approach, took to the skies leaving branches quivering in their wake. There was nothing they could catch, and Agesilaus seemed keen to cover as much distance as possible. He bounded on ahead, sometimes breaking into a slow run. A little after midday, Demaratos fell into step alongside Lysander. He was still hobbling a little, and the bandage over his cut was black with dust and blood.

'Where do you think he's taking us?' he asked. 'Sparta must be more than a day's march away now.'

'I don't know,' replied Lysander. 'But this is the final day. I'm sure it will be something difficult.'

Soon Lysander could hear the babble of running water in the distance, and it reminded him of his thirst. He'd been rationing the water from the settlement, and was longing to wash the filth from his body.

'I'm almost missing Diokles,' joked Demaratos, and Lysander couldn't help but laugh. Agesilaus stopped ahead.

'Is something funny?' he said with menace. 'It's time for the final test – you must prove yourselves hunters. Fish, bird, and beast. Before we can return to Sparta, you must kill one of each. We'll reach the river soon.'

'I can catch a fish easily,' boasted Demaratos. 'My father taught me when I was small.'

'How?' asked Lysander. 'We haven't even got a line, or a hook . . .'

'Wait and see,' said Demaratos. They reached some rocks at the edge of a small valley. Far below, a river cut through the landscape. It was flowing fast. In places, the water churned noisily in crests of white foam, or else it slid over flat polished rocks. There were deep pools too, and Lysander could see right through the clear water to the bottom.

'Look!' shouted Demaratos. 'Fish. Lots of them!'

He was right. Even from this height, Lysander could see several fish, their bodies black and sleek as they hung in the strong current.

Demaratos headed down the slope, upsetting small

rocks and dust with his heels. Lysander set off in pursuit. Even with a net it would be difficult to catch any fish. And the water was flowing too fast to climb in. It would sweep a person off their feet.

They soon reached the water's edge. The water here was quite still and, crouching beside the river, Lysander scooped great handfuls of the cool clear liquid into his mouth and threw it over his head and neck, washing away the grime that had collected there. When his belly could hold no more water, he started filling his flask.

'There's no time to waste,' shouted Agesilaus. 'You have a task to fulfil. Get to it!'

Lysander and Demaratos stood on the bank. At the top of the pool, where the water gushed between two flat rocks, several fish had gathered, their noses turned into the current.

'See that fat one on the left,' said Demaratos, pointing. 'He's mine!'

'Show us then,' said Agesilaus, folding his arms with a sneer.

Demaratos walked slowly up the bank, crouching low and keeping his eyes on the fish. Lysander was reminded of watching him wrestling in the exercise yard, circling his opponent. He reached the head of their section of the river, where several large boulders were scattered through the middle of the river. He took off his sandals and clambered on to one of the boulders. One misplaced foot, and he would plunge into the water below, where the current was strongest.

Eddies swirled over the sharp rocks below. Lysander wanted to call for him to be careful, but didn't want to disturb the fish.

Agesilaus came to stand beside Lysander.

'He should take care,' he said. 'Or he'll be food for the fish.'

Demaratos hopped from one rock to the next, steadying himself with his outstretched arms. To get to the next rock, he had to place his feet into the water. He lowered himself. *He's feeling for a firm foothold*, thought Lysander. With both feet under the surface, Lysander could see that Demaratos's knuckles were white where he was still gripping the rock he had descended from. With a lunge he pushed himself off and reached for the rock ahead. As he left his anchor, his feet slipped and he let out a cry.

'Told you,' said Agesilaus.

Demaratos clung to the rock, and regained his feet. Lysander could see that the muscles in his arms were trembling with the effort of holding on.

After the danger, he made his way to the centre of the river quickly and safely. He knelt down on a flat rock a little above the surface of the rapids below. Demaratos lowered his hands very slowly into the water, his eyes focused downwards.

'This is ridiculous,' said Agesilaus.

Lysander crept further up the bank to get a closer look. The big fish hadn't moved. It still lay almost motionless, twitching its muscular tail to keep itself steady. Why didn't it swim away? Lysander wondered. Surely it could see Demaratos moving his hands ever closer?

Lysander watched as Demaratos placed his hands underneath the fish. He stayed in that same position for some time. Lysander found himself holding his breath. A bead of sweat dropped from Demaratos's forehead into the water. Even Agesilaus had crept closer to watch.

'What's he doing?' Lysander asked him. 'Why doesn't he grab it?'

'I don't know,' replied Agesilaus gruffly. 'He's more stupid than an Athenian if he thinks the fish is going to jump into his hands.'

Demaratos suddenly whipped his hands out of the water. There was a flash of silver as the fish came out as well, spiralling high into the air, and landing on the bank near to Lysander. The speckled trout flopped around and then lay still on its side, its mouth working open and closed. Demaratos stood on his rock and gave a whoop of joy.

'I told you I could do it!' he yelled. 'I told you.'

'How did you manage it?' shouted back Lysander.

'I was tickling it,' said Demaratos. 'It sends them into a sort of trance. They fall asleep in the water.' He was looking down near his feet. 'Wait! I see another. This one's twice as big!'

Demaratos was on his knees again, placing his hands back in the water. Lysander couldn't see much of the fish – it looked like a dark shadow under the water. But it was a big shadow. Two fish would feed them well.

Demaratos tickled for longer this time – Lysander guessed he wanted to be sure before he tried to bring the fish out. Then, with the same jerking motion the fish came up in his hands. The trout was glistening in the sunshine; it was longer than his forearm. But as Demaratos lifted it from the water, it squirmed from his grasp. He'd made a mistake – the fish hadn't fallen asleep. Demaratos leant out further to try and grab it. Too far. As the fish arched out of his reach, Demaratos toppled into the raging torrent.

'No!' Lysander called out. But it was too late. Demaratos had disappeared under the water.

CHAPTER 11

Demaratos dragged his head above the current.

'Help! Hel—' His shouts were stifled as he was pulled back under.

Lysander readied himself to plunge into the water, but Demaratos was already past him. He set off after Agesilaus along the bank. Demaratos reached the end of the main pool and was sucked towards a chute of rapids flowing over shallow rocks. His body disappeared quickly over the edge.

'Swim to the bank!' shouted Lysander, but he could see it was hopeless – the current was too strong. Rounding the set of rocks on dry land, he watched as Demaratos scrambled furiously to get a hold of something on the bank. But the stones there were green with slippery algae, and his hands couldn't find any grip along the smooth surfaces.

Lysander threw himself on his belly over a rock and stretched out over the water. 'Here, Demaratos!'

Demaratos reached out a hand, but his wet fingers

slipped from Lysander's grasp. He wasn't shouting now, and Lysander could see the fear in his face as he continued downstream. Lysander climbed quickly to his feet. Ahead of him, Agesilaus reached a weeping willow tree, its slender branches sagging into the water. He pulled something from his belt – a dagger – and quickly cut off one of the branches. Demaratos flailed in the powerful water.

Agesilaus leapt on to a boulder and held out the branch.

'Demaratos!' he yelled. 'Grab this!'

Demaratos reached out. *Come on*, willed Lysander. *You can do it. Just a little further.* His hands closed around the branch. Agesilaus was lying on his stomach, anchored in place. All Demaratos had to do was pull himself towards the bank. But the older boy wasn't helping. Why wasn't he tugging on the branch to bring Demaratos to safety?

'Pull him up!' Lysander shouted. Then he saw that Agesilaus was smiling. The blond-haired Spartan slowly loosened his grip and allowed the branch to slip from his fingers.

'No!' yelled Lysander. Demaratos was in the river's grasp once again. 'What are you doing?' cried Lysander.

Agesilaus laughed. 'Better get after him, don't you think?'

Lysander wanted to slam his fist into the Spartan's face. But if they didn't get Demaratos out of the water, he'd either drown, or some submerged rock would smash open his skull.

Lysander ran down the bank and shouted to Demaratos.

'Get on your back. Go feet first, it'll protect your head.' He watched as Demaratos struggled into position. If he met any obstacles now, his legs would bear the brunt. A broken or torn leg was better than a head wound. Demaratos seemed to be trying to say something, and was making gestures with his arms, but Lysander couldn't understand what he meant. He heard one word – 'bridge'. He looked up and saw it. Thirty paces away – a small wooden platform spanning the river where it narrowed. Lysander took off, crashing through the bushes and branches that covered the river bank, his feet sliding in the mud. He reached the bridge before Demaratos. Beneath the planks the river channel narrowed and fell away in a waterfall. The cascade was as tall as five men, and the pool below was shallow. Jagged rocks broke the surface of the water. If Demaratos went over, he was almost certain to be killed, his body smashed and torn.

'Better hurry and help your friend!' shouted Agesilaus from upstream.

Lysander lay on his front and reached down towards the water below. But he was still an arm's length above the torrent. *I've got to get closer!* There was only one way. Hooking his feet behind the wooden posts on the far side of the bridge, he lowered his whole upper body over the other, taking the strain on his ankles.

Demaratos's face contorted with terror. He began desperately paddling against the current, but the river was too strong and dragged him on.

Lysander would only get one chance. As Demaratos came towards him, he reached as far as he could over the edge of the bridge, his fingers straining. Demaratos crashed into him. Lysander grabbed him under the armpits and locked his fingers together.

Immediately, he was pulled along with Demaratos, and his feet jarred against the posts of the bridge. Pain tore through his muscles.

'Don't let me go! Don't let me drown!' sobbed Demaratos. The current blasted over him, spraying into his eyes.

Lysander heaved on Demaratos's body, and managed to lift his friend out of the water but the pressure in his back was excruciating and his arms felt as though they'd be pulled from their sockets. Demaratos could do nothing but hang; he didn't have the strength to heave himself upwards. Lysander's feet were slipping from around the posts and his body slid further towards the water. He knew he couldn't hold on for long.

'We have to work together,' he shouted over the roar of the water.

Demaratos kicked hard with his feet. Lysander gritted his teeth and tugged. At first nothing, but then Demaratos began to come up. He kept on kicking, and the slight release of pressure gave Lysander hope. They could make it. He heaved again, until his joints screamed in pain. Demaratos managed to swing his arm and grab the edge of the bridge. Lysander grabbed his waist and roughly pulled Demaratos on to the platform. They'd done it! Lysander rolled on to his back, as Demaratos gasped for breath beside him.

'Have you two finished lazing around?' said Agesilaus, wandering casually across the bridge and standing over them.

'I could have been killed!' said Demaratos. He made a grab at the older boy's legs, but fell short, collapsing back on to the bridge.

'I always knew that Lysander here would save you,' said Agesilaus. 'Anyhow, you needed a bath.' He held up the fish. 'Come on, let's eat your catch and get going.'

Lysander and Demaratos were still soaked to the skin as they headed back to the water's edge, each carrying a bundle of firewood.

'I can't wait to pay him back,' said Demaratos, his dark hair plastered to his head.

'Be careful,' said Lysander. 'He's got a knife.'

'What?' said Demaratos. 'We're not allowed weapons.'

'I saw him pull it out to cut a branch.'

'What a cheat!' said Demaratos.

When they reached the riverside, Agesilaus was sharpening a stick with the knife.

'Get a fire going!' he ordered. 'It's nearly midday and

we've hardly begun today's task.'

As Demaratos arranged the wood over some dried leaves and flakes of bark, Lysander took out his flint. Agesilaus placed the trout on a rock and ran the blade under the speckled belly. He scooped out the guts and threw them in the bushes. Lysander kindled the fire while Agesilaus cleaned the carcass at the water's edge. Then he took the sharpened stick and skewered the dead fish, resting it over the fire's low flame.

'I thought we were supposed to survive by our wits out here,' asked Lysander. 'Why do you have a knife?'

'I never go anywhere without it,' said Agesilaus.

But why keep the knife a secret?

The skin of the fish was turning brown and crispy over the fire.

'This knife is my key to the Krypteia,' said Agesilaus.

Demaratos suddenly looked interested.

'What do you mean?' he asked.

Agesilaus turned the fish to cook the other side.

'I'm nearly old enough to join,' he said. 'But first one has to pass a test.'

'What test?' asked Demaratos.

Agesilaus grinned. 'They make you carry out three assassinations. If you get caught, you have failed the test.'

Lysander was in no mood to hear about the Krypteia and moved to one of the rocks by the river.

'Have you . . . have you killed anybody?' he heard Demaratos ask.

Agesilaus snorted. 'Of course I have – with this very knife in fact.'

Lysander turned and saw Agesilaus holding the dagger in the sunlight. The blade was dull and worn, about the distance from Lysander's wrist to the tip of his finger. It was wide at the bottom, with edges curving to a sharp point. The handle was simple pale wood. Lysander looked back towards the river.

'Who?' asked Demaratos.

Agesilaus made a show of hesitating. 'I suppose you're old enough to know,' he eventually said, before continuing with his story. 'They don't tell you the names. It's always a Helot. They point them out: a face in a crowd, or a house. It's up to the trainee to stalk his prey and do the deed in secret.'

He's pathetic, thought Lysander. *He wants to boast, that's all.* But Lysander couldn't ignore the creeping feeling of tension that prickled his skin. Agesilaus had killed a Helot? Now he strained to hear more.

'How many have you killed?' asked Demaratos, with awe in his voice.

'Two, so far,' replied the older boy. 'The first was a man from a settlement near the village of Sellasia. He was drunk when I followed him from a friend's house – you know the home-brewed wines these Helots like – but still he put up quite a fight. I only managed to cut his arm at first, and we ended up rolling on the floor. He was strong, but slow through the drink. He did manage to hit me on the head with a rock, but by that stage he was bleeding badly from all the times I'd stuck him. I went home covered in blood – not my own, thank the Gods. Ah, the fish is ready!'

Lysander sat back down beside the two others, as Agesilaus divided the trout into three portions on a bed of fern leaves. Steam rose up from the fish's pink flesh. He gave himself the largest piece.

'And the second victim?' asked Lysander, reaching out for his food.

Agesilaus swallowed a mouthful of fish and licked his fingers.

'The second was very different,' he said. 'It was after the night when we made the Helots pay for their insolence – just before we left for the hills, in fact. The night the streets ran red. It was after dawn, a difficult time to carry out a killing. With my mentor, Pylades, we waited for most of the Helots to head out to the fields, then entered the settlement secretly. Pylades pointed to a certain house, and told me to kill every male inside. I was happy – if I could kill two, my apprenticeship would be complete.'

'Did you do it?' asked Demaratos. Lysander was finding it difficult to eat – he could barely stand to listen to Agesilaus' story, but at the same time he had to know.

'There was only one,' said Agesilaus with a shrug. 'Not what I was expecting at all. I crept through the front door, and found no one. The place was a stinking hovel – these Helots live no better than animals. But in

111

the back room there was a figure asleep on a bed. There was a bucket of water and a bloody cloth on the floor beside him; perhaps he was one of those flogged the night before. I drew closer and saw his sleeping face. Well, he was only a boy. Maybe your age or even younger.'

Lysander was watching Agesilaus as he spoke. Each word sent sparks through Lysander's brain. He thought about Timeon's body, growing cold in his mother's house.

'I took out this knife,' continued Agesilaus, holding the blade up. The sunlight caught his fair hair, as he stared at the weapon. 'I placed my hand over his mouth, and I jammed the blade between his ribs.' Lysander looked at the blade again – just long enough to penetrate the heart. His head spun as the words washed over him. 'He struggled, but I twisted the blade and he went limp. He wouldn't have suffered long.'

'You killed a boy?' said Demaratos with a frown. Lysander put down his fish.

Agesilaus leant back on his arms. 'I did,' he said, re-sheathing the dagger. 'They were my orders, and I wasn't going to let a worthless Helot stand in my way.'

Rage coursed through Lysander as he got to his feet. Agesilaus looked up at him.

'What? Have I offended your Helot blood?'

'You murderer,' Lysander muttered. He threw himself at Agesilaus, knocking him backwards, and pummelling him with his fists.

'Get off me!' shouted the older boy.

Agesilaus tried to defend himself as Lysander rained down blows. He could feel the older boy's sharp cheekbones under his knuckles and noticed that the skin of Agesilaus' face had split open. But this wasn't enough to stop him. 'I'll kill you!' he shouted over and over. Then he felt Demaratos dragging him away.

'What's got into you?' said Demaratos. 'You're behaving like an animal!'

Lysander spat in Agesilaus' direction, fury still throbbing through his body. 'He's the animal!'

Agesilaus grabbed his knife, his skin flushed with anger.

'I'll gut you like a fish, Helot.'

CHAPTER 12

'No!' said Demaratos.

Lysander felt his companion's grip loosen and pulled himself free. He aimed a kick at the embers of the fire, scattering ash and burning embers towards Agesilaus. The Spartan stumbled backwards with a cry and Lysander charged at him. The knife flew from his hand as Agesilaus crashed to the ground. Lysander leapt at him and grabbed the older boy's throat.

'You murdered my friend!' he spat, smashing Agesilaus' head on to the ground. 'By the Gods, I'll kill you.'

Agesilaus' hands were clawing at Lysander. He squeezed harder still, and Agesilaus' eyes began to bulge. Demaratos was behind him, trying to pull him off, but Lysander refused to let go. He was going to throttle the life out of Timeon's killer. Agesilaus' face turned from red to purple and his hands fell by his side. Spittle caught at the corners of his mouth, as he tried to draw a breath. A moment of clarity entered Lysander's mind:

Carry on like this and he'll die. Do you want a second death on your conscience? Lysander started to loosen his grip. But Agesilaus' fainting fit had been a ruse. He lunged to grab his knife and swung the blade at Lysander, who just had time to rear away. The knife grazed his neck, and clattered to the ground. Agesilaus was taken over by a coughing fit, the breath returning to his lungs. He writhed in the dirt, too weak to stand.

Demaratos limped forwards and crouched beside him. Agesilaus looked pathetic as he knelt in the dirt, gasping for air, his chest heaving. Lysander climbed to his feet. The fight was over.

'Are you all right?' asked Demaratos. Agesilaus roughly pushed him away, too proud to accept sympathy. He stood slowly and turned, rubbing his throat with one hand. He retrieved his knife and brandished it towards Lysander. His face was still red and his eyes bloodshot.

'You tried to kill me,' he said.

Now the older boy was tossing his dagger from hand to hand.

'Feel free to return the favour,' Lysander said. The older boy looked surprised and he missed catching the knife. It fell to the ground. Agesilaus swooped down and retrieved it for a second time. Lysander saw his grip tighten on the hilt. So this was it.

'Wait! What's that?' said Demaratos. He was pointing behind Lysander. In the distance, several columns of grey smoke curled into the air. 'Forest fire!'

'Quick, we have to go and see,' said Agesilaus. He stuffed the dagger back into his belt, shooting a warning glance in Lysander's direction. Then he set off towards the bridge. Demaratos kicked over the remaining embers of their fire, and followed. Agesilaus turned back from the bridge to look at Lysander.

'This isn't over, Lysander – you'll pay for what you did. Maybe not today, but soon. You had better sleep with one eye open from now on.'

Lysander could see the smoke billowing over the horizon. His thighs burned as he climbed the steep cliff. He had already overtaken the other two. If there was a forest fire, the sooner they took the news back to Sparta the better. The crops might still be saved if people could be organised in time. He clambered up the slope on the far side of the river, feeling for hand-holds and hauling his body from rock to rock.

But as they came closer, his instincts told him this was no forest fire. The smoke was separated into columns, as though there were lots of small fires.

Finally he reached the top of the mountain, where the wind whipped around him. The view was astonishing. The hill fell away in a series of rocky ridges to the plain below. Lysander could see the river Eurotas like a silver snake as it meandered through the wide valley, all the way to the expanse of water beyond. The smoke rose from behind a low headland near the sea.

116

Lysander had never seen the Great Sea before. It took his breath away. The water shone as blue as the sky, fringed with flashes of gold in the afternoon sun. But that wasn't all. Riding the waves were warships, perhaps a hundred, painted red and black. The ones furthest from shore had their square white sails unfurled. The smoke was coming from the shoreline. Lysander heard Agesilaus and Demaratos scramble up behind him.

'That's no forest fire,' said Agesilaus. 'The smoke is above the harbour villages – they've been set ablaze!'

'What? Who do those ships belong to?' asked Demaratos, breathing heavily.

'Persian triremes!' said Agesilaus. 'Dozens of them!' For the first time ever, he sounded impressed.

Lysander watched in silence as the ships, with their prows and two layers of oars looming out of the water, headed for the shore. The sound of the drums from the ships – meant to keep the rowers in time – boomed up the valley.

As he watched, Lysander made out pinpricks of fire over the decks of one of the leading Persian vessels.

'Archers!' said Agesilaus. Lysander's heart thumped in his chest as the flaming arrows sailed through the air, before descending to the shore out of sight. He felt completely powerless.

'No . . .' he mumbled beneath his breath. He could imagine the flames springing up through the town. Thank the Gods he couldn't hear the people's screams.

Suddenly, further inland, a lone rider burst from the trees by the river, galloping north towards Sparta, his red cloak billowing on the wind. Two more riders appeared in pursuit, one carrying a short spear, the other with a bow slung over his shoulder. Lysander could tell from their colourful, baggy clothes and dark skins that they weren't Greeks.

'He must be a messenger,' said Demaratos. 'He's gone to warn the Spartans about the attack.'

The Persians were closing on the solitary Spartan rider, and when they were ten lengths behind, the spearman released his weapon. Lysander could just see it bury itself in the top of the horse's leg. The animal crumpled to the ground, sending the rider headlong on to the path. The man quickly regained his feet and drew his sword, but the Persians were now out of range. The other rider slowly unslung his bow and pulled an arrow from his quiver. The archer casually strung the arrow, drew the string, and released. It was strange watching the fight from so high above. No sound reached Lysander's ears. The Spartan soldier fell backwards, with the arrow through his head. He twitched on the ground.

'Cowards,' said Demaratos.

'We have to get back to Sparta,' said Lysander. 'Without the messenger, the city won't know of the danger.'

Agesilaus stood in his way. 'We can't go back yet,' he

said. 'You haven't finished your task.'

Lysander looked at Agesilaus in astonishment, then pointed towards the sea.

'Can't you see what's happening? War is on the threshold of our city, and you talk of tasks? The first boats will be on the beaches, unloading soldiers. They'll kill innocent people: Helots and free-dwellers alike. We must go back now!'

Agesilaus drew himself up.

'You'll do as I say!' he shouted. 'You must complete the Ordeal. A bird and a beast!'

'This is ridiculous,' said Lysander. 'You'd have us stand by while Sparta is attacked?'

A fleeting look of uncertainty passed over Agesilaus' face, and for a moment Lysander thought he'd got through to him. But Agesilaus suddenly charged forward, tripping him to the floor. He knelt on Lysander's chest and put the dagger to his throat. Lysander hardly dared to swallow with the blade pressed so tightly to his skin.

'Do you really think Sparta needs a Helot half-breed like you fighting her cause? What could you do to prevent a war? The army will deal with those Persians like they were swatting flies.'

'Stop!' said Demaratos, and Lysander saw his hand on Agesilaus' shoulder. 'If you hurt him, you'll have to kill me too.' Agesilaus turned and looked towards Demaratos. 'You won't look very good leaving the mountains on your own, will you?'

Lysander wondered for a moment whether Agesilaus might simply kill them both on the spot, but he climbed off Lysander's chest.

'Sparta will be fine,' he said more calmly. 'There are maybe three thousand men in that attack – our army is thirty thousand strong and better trained. We'll finish the Ordeal and head back tomorrow.'

'But what about the people on the shoreline?' said Lysander.

Agesilaus grinned, and sheathed his dagger.

'They're only free-dwellers and Helots. Let them die.'

Lysander led the way back down the mountain. Sparta was a full day's walk on the valley floor, but they couldn't risk going that way in case the Persians sent out scouts. They'd have to stick to the mountain route and drop back into the city the way they had left. Demaratos caught up with Lysander, wincing a little on his bad leg, and fell into step beside him.

'What do you think the Persians will do?' he asked.

'I don't know,' Lysander replied. 'They'll gather their forces tonight and make camp, I expect. It's too late to attack now. Maybe they'll wait a day before launching their attack, maybe not.'

'Their attack?' said Demaratos, breathing heavily.

'Of course,' said Lysander. 'They may strike at dawn,

or perhaps the following night.'

'Lysander, my family are in Sparta, we have to get back soon,' said Demaratos.

'But first we have to fulfil these senseless tasks,' Lysander replied. 'You heard Agesilaus – I think he'd rather kill us than break the rules of the Ordeal.'

Several birds were startled out of the tree ahead and scattered into the air, settling in a tree further down the slope.

'I have an idea,' said Lysander. He took the sling from his belt, and scooped several stones from the ground, loading them into the leather pouch.

'You'll never be able to hit a bird with that thing,' Agesilaus called from behind them.

'Maybe I can't hit one bird,' muttered Lysander. 'But I have a chance if there are lots. Stay here, and come when you see my signal.'

He made his way back up the slope, past Agesilaus. He headed along the ridge and descended beyond the tree where the birds were resting, hiding himself behind a boulder. He could see Demaratos and Agesilaus waiting and waved for them to come down the path. As they walked, kicking up gravel, the birds lifted from their perches, then wheeled in the sky and flew in Lysander's direction. He swung the sling and released a volley of pebbles. Most missed their targets, but one bird flapped clumsily in the air, and then plummeted to the ground. Lysander reached the fallen bird at the same time as Agesilaus and

121

Demaratos. It wasn't quite dead, and moved one black wing slowly up and down as though trying to fly.

'It's a swift,' said Demaratos. 'They fly through at this time of year.'

A small trickle of blood was flowing from the bird's beak. Lysander picked up the bird carefully, supporting its body and its brown-hooded head. The short feathers of its belly were white and fluffy. With a quick wrenching movement, he snapped its neck and dropped the bird to the ground.

'That's one down,' he said matter-of-factly. 'Only a beast to go.'

Agesilaus grunted and gave a small nod. Demaratos grinned. Lysander didn't have time to feel remorse. They continued walking in silence until they reached the river.

'Lysander, I'm sorry about Timeon,' said Demaratos. 'He was a good slave.' Lysander shot him a look. 'And a good person,' Demaratos added hastily.

They covered ground quickly and reached their old shelter under the cliff face as the sun was setting, extinguishing their long shadows. Agesilaus called them to a halt.

'We'll sleep here tonight,' he said. 'There's no use trying to hunt until morning.'

Lysander tried to make himself comfortable on the rough ground, but he knew he wouldn't be able to sleep. Not while the Persians amassed their forces near the shore. Someone had to warn Sparta. Lysander felt fierce loyalty and realised that, Spartan or Helot, one thing was for sure. He wanted to save his home.

CHAPTER 13

Lysander lay in the darkness, listening to his companions' breathing. In his hand he held the carving that Timeon's mother had given him. *What should I do, Timeon? Stay here?* He closed his eyes and let his fingers move over the ridges in the wood. Why were they wasting time in the mountains when they could be helping their countrymen? It was just like a Spartan to put tradition before all else. Even common sense.

Despite Agesilaus' confidence, Lysander wasn't so sure of the Spartan defences. Even if the Persians were beaten, how many of his comrades would be killed first? Sarpedon's words echoed in his head: 'Remember all you have learnt, obey Agesilaus, and work together.' Would his grandfather have said that if he had seen Agesilaus' behaviour in the mountains? Lysander didn't think so.

No, he told himself, *I'm not going to lie here*. Lysander knew what he had to do.

He got to his feet. Stepping into the pale glow of the moonlight, a tingle of fear prickled the length of his spine. *What if Agesilaus wakes? Will he try to follow me?* Lysander looked at where the older boy lay. He was on his side, facing the rocks. In his belt, the hilt of his dagger gleamed. His only weapon. Could Lysander risk taking it?

He crept back towards the Spartan. Agesilaus didn't stir. Crouching down, Lysander reached towards the dagger. His fingers were shaking. *Concentrate*, he told himself. He took a deep breath, closing one hand around the hilt. He steadied the sheath with his other hand. Slowly, he pulled. The dagger slipped out smoothly, without a sound. Lysander stood up, weighing the blade in his palm. Agesilaus wasn't half as dangerous any more. He tucked the knife into his own belt, with the blade pointing downwards. It was time to go.

Lysander felt liberated as soon as the shelter was out of sight. On his first day in the mountains, he wouldn't have dared even look the wrong way at Agesilaus. Now he was stealing his knife and disobeying his orders. But he'd learnt so much, about himself and the others. He had seized his destiny and survived.

If he moved quickly, he could be in Sparta before dawn. He imagined Agesilaus waking to find him gone. He'd be furious, and might blame Demaratos, but Lysander couldn't worry about that now. Demaratos could look after himself.

He reached a clearing in the trees. Something rustled ahead. He stopped in his tracks and drew the dagger, scanning the bushes for any signs of life. Lysander watched as a shadow passed between the trees ahead. It was bigger than a wild boar. Had Agesilaus come to cut him off?

'Come out,' said Lysander, trying to control the tremor in his voice. The shadow stopped dead. Lysander hid the knife behind his back.

'I know it's you, Agesilaus.'

The shadow moved again, and something emerged from behind the tree. It wasn't Agesilaus. A long grey snout, catching flecks of silver in the moonlight. A wolf. Lysander gripped the knife more tightly in his hand, feeling his pulse quicken, and glanced all around him. He'd heard wolves hunted in packs, but this one seemed to be alone. It sloped out from its hiding place, feet padding softly in the pine needles that littered the ground. Its black lip twitched upwards, revealing pointed white teeth. A low snarl escaped its mouth. Its eyes, like molten discs, fixed on Lysander.

Lysander started to back off, facing the wolf. It moved slowly forward, giving a low growl. Lysander could see by its lean body that it must be hungry. There was no way he could outrun the animal. If he turned his back, it would tear him apart.

Lysander dropped into a crouch, moving into a fighting stance. The wolf drew its lips back over purple gums. Another deep, loud growl filled the clearing, and the hackles lifted across its back. The hairs on Lysander's own neck rose. There was only one choice: fight. He adjusted the dagger so the blade pointed downwards along his forearm for a better grip.

The wolf pounced, the weight of fur and claws crashing into him. Lysander cried out and put up his arms to protect himself. As he hit the ground, the knife sliced into the top of the wolf's leg and it dropped back with a whimper. Blood dripped across the ground, glistening in the moonlight.

Lysander scrambled back to his feet, but the wolf leapt at him again, its forepaws on his chest as its open jaws reached up and snapped at his throat. Lysander threw the creature to one side, slashing with the knife, and stumbled backwards. The blade clattered to the ground. Lysander staggered to his feet and looked desperately for the knife, but he couldn't see it anywhere in the darkness. The wolf came more slowly this time, and Lysander aimed a kick at its neck. The beast moved to one side, easily dodging the blow, and snarled again, lowering its head. Lysander was breathing hard. Something was trickling down his arm. Blood.

He looked around frantically for an escape. Then his eyes caught a shape on the horizon – a boy.

'Demaratos?' he shouted. 'Help me!' The silhouette didn't move. *Agesilaus?* 'Please!' Lysander yelled. 'It's going to kill me!'

The wolf licked its teeth, and circled. *It's toying with*

me, Lysander realised. Then he saw it: a low branch stuck out from a tree a few paces behind the wolf. If he could only reach it, perhaps he could climb out of danger.

The wolf flattened its ears again, ready to pounce. Lysander kicked out, showering the wolf with dirt and dust. It was the distraction he needed. He dashed towards the tree, not looking back. He could hear the scratch of the wolf's paws on the ground behind him. Lysander reached the tree and jumped for the branch. As his fingers closed around the wood he pulled his weight up. But at the same time there was a crunch. *No!* The branch was rotten, and fell away from the tree. Lysander fell with it.

The wolf was on him before he could think, and Lysander could smell the savagery on its breath. His vision was filled with flashing eyes and snapping teeth. Lysander could hear his own cries of terror. His mind was telling him one thing: survive. But the wolf was strong. Pain ripped through him as the wolf's jaws closed on his left forearm. Then he felt something under his right hand. Wood. His fingers closed around the branch, and he swung it as hard as he could. He connected and the wolf yelped, releasing his arm. He struck again, and the wolf's forelegs collapsed. It was still lying on him, but its bloodied mouth hung open, dazed. Lysander adjusted his grip on the wood and aimed the tip at the wolf's head, towards his eyes. Lysander hesitated, and then he pushed.

The tip of the stake entered the glossy eyeball to a finger's length, and the wolf gave a strange curdled breath through its teeth. Lysander brought his other hand around the staff and thrust it further into the socket. The beast went completely stiff, a whimper dying in its throat. Three spasms followed, each weaker than the one before. Then the wolf was still.

Lysander sank back, gasping for air beneath the heavy bulk of the dead wolf. As the relief drained, he felt like laughing and crying at the same time. His arm was bloody and covered with puncture marks; blood trickled down his neck from a gash somewhere on his cheek.

Another howl pierced the air, and Lysander struggled to sit up. But it wasn't a wolf. The figure that he'd seen on the horizon stepped down from his vantage point. Lysander heard the crunch of his feet as he stepped through the shadows into the clearing. Then he moved into a patch of light. The blond hair looked white under the moon. Agesilaus.

'Why didn't you help me?' said Lysander.

Agesilaus didn't speak, but bent to the ground and picked something up. The dagger. He walked towards Lysander with a sneer of contempt on his lips.

'It looks like you managed to kill this old wolf.'

'Yes,' said Lysander. There was an odd look in Agesilaus' face. His eyes were cold as ice.

'Let's see where the rest of the pack are.'

His hands were cupped under his mouth, and he let

out a howl into the night air.

'Are you mad?' asked Lysander.

Agesilaus raised his eyebrows.

'You shouldn't have run away, Lysander. My orders were to stay at the shelter until morning.'

Lysander had to think fast.

'I heard the wolf – I was only trying to complete the Ordeal.'

'You're lying, Lysander. You were leaving us.' The look in his eyes was pitiless, deadly. 'You stole my knife too. I told you never to steal my weapon again.'

The night air suddenly became very cold.

'Where's Demaratos?' asked Lysander.

'He's still sleeping,' replied Agesilaus. 'It's just you and me now.'

The futility of the situation suddenly overwhelmed Lysander. He couldn't help his anger. 'You should have led us down yourself,' he shouted. 'Sparta's in danger.'

Agesilaus smiled and shook his head. 'You still don't understand, do you, Lysander?'

'Understand what?'

'The reason we couldn't leave so soon.'

In the pause that followed, the truth came to Lysander – the climb down the treacherous rocks for peppermint leaves, the night in the freezing snow, Agesilaus goading him at the river's edge.

'I wasn't supposed to ever go back, was I?' he said.

Agesilaus snorted a laugh. 'You've made enemies,

mothax, and even your grandfather isn't powerful enough to protect you. Let's just say my orders were to make things . . . difficult for you. Very difficult.'

'What are you going to do?' asked Lysander, trying to push the wolf's corpse off himself. 'Kill me?'

Agesilaus laughed. 'No, Lysander, *I'm* not going to kill you.' He nodded above Lysander with his head. 'They are.'

Lysander twisted on the ground and looked. On the top of the cliffs, three wolves, drawn by Agesilaus' call, were silhouetted against the sky. The older boy let out another howl, and the animals ran fluidly down the hill.

'Farewell, Lysander. I'll tell your grandfather you died like a coward.' He sheathed his knife, and leant down, smiling. 'Don't wake Demaratos with your screams.'

'Too late,' said a voice.

Lysander saw a rock strike the side of the Spartan's head, and a look of confusion crossed his face. Then Agesilaus stumbled and collapsed. Demaratos hobbled quickly over and started pulling the wolf's carcass off Lysander's chest. Lysander did his best to help, pushing the bloodied and matted body off him, trying not to gag at the scent of the wild animal.

'Come on!' said Demaratos, offering his hand. 'The wolves are coming.'

Lysander took his arm and climbed to his feet.

Agesilaus was on all fours, trying to shake his head clear.

'I'll kill you both like Helot swine!' he shouted. The knife was back in his hand.

Lysander saw the first wolf enter the clearing behind Agesilaus. He yanked Demaratos towards him.

Agesilaus spun around, but it was too late. The wolf flew through the air and sank its teeth in his arm. The Spartan screamed and tried to punch the wolf, but it kept its grip. Lysander saw a second wolf break cover. They'd all be dead soon.

'We need to climb!' shouted Lysander, scanning the clearing. If they could get into a tree, they might survive.

'There!' said Demaratos, pointing to a large boulder at the base of a clump of trees. As Agesilaus fought with the first wolf, its mate tore at the back of his leg. He collapsed to one knee, and a howl escaped his lips. Lysander leapt on to the boulder behind Demaratos, who was already pulling himself into the branches above as a third wolf darted across towards the boulder.

Lysander had one hand on the branch as the wolf bounded up behind him. It tried to come for his legs, but he managed to swing them out of the way as the teeth snapped at his shins. Demaratos grabbed him from above and heaved him up into the tree.

'Thanks,' gasped Lysander. The wolf snarled below, but it couldn't reach them.

Agesilaus writhed in the middle of the clearing, his free hand clawing at the wolf that was tearing at his leg, but it was useless. The third wolf jumped down from the boulder and sank its teeth into the side of Agesilaus' neck. Blood spattered across its fur and the older boy's cry of agony made Lysander's blood run cold.

'I can't watch,' said Demaratos, turning his head away.

But Lysander forced his eyes to stay on the scene of slaughter. Agesilaus had killed his friend. Now he would suffer, too. Agesilaus twisted on the ground, letting out a weak moan. The wolf at his neck released him, and the others followed suit, letting his body fall from their jaws. Their interest was waning; the attack was over. They stood over his prone figure, their chests rising and falling as their breathing misted the air.

One at a time, they left the Spartan lying in the dust, and loped away into the trees. One of them ran over towards the dead wolf and nuzzled its fur. Then it turned and disappeared into the dark. Lysander watched the shapes of the three wolves merge with the forest shadows. Then they were gone.

Lysander and Demaratos waited in the tree as silence settled over the clearing.

'Let's go down,' said Lysander. 'They're not coming back.'

Demaratos nodded. They lowered themselves on to

the boulder and climbed down. Walking towards Agesilaus' body, Lysander could see there was a great deal of blood on the ground. One of Agesilaus' hands twitched.

'May the Gods have pity on him,' whispered Demaratos. 'The wolves must have attacked him for sport.'

Lysander approached Agesilaus. His face was a ghostly white and flecked with blood, his breathing shallow. The side of his throat was almost completely ripped away, revealing the glistening red muscle beneath. His lips moved, but no sound emerged apart from a gurgle of blood. His half-closed eyelids fluttered. The only sound was the breath rattling through Agesilaus' chest.

Lysander crouched down beside the body.

'Can't we help him?' said Demaratos.

'It's too late,' said Lysander.

Agesilaus' eyes flickered open.

'Lysan . . .' he croaked.

'He wants to say something to you,' said Demaratos.

Lysander lowered his ear to Agesilaus' mouth. Would he apologise with his last breath? *Can I forgive him?*

Agesilaus' breathing was coming in short gasps now.

'Helot scum,' he whispered. He didn't take another breath.

Lysander's face tightened as he got to his feet.

'What did he say?' Demaratos asked.

As the light dimmed in Agesilaus' eyes, Lysander turned to Demaratos.

'It's not important.' He looked back down at the boy who had been his tormentor. 'A beast is dead.'

CHAPTER 14

The birds began their song with first light.

Lysander led the way down from the mountain, hurrying along the path as dawn broke over the hills to the east. His feet were soaked by the dew, but he didn't care; it washed away the blood. He and Demaratos were returning home, leaving behind the mountains, and death. He had faced the test of a true Spartan. He had completed the Ordeal, killing fish, bird and beast. He'd entered the mountains a boy; he was leaving them a man.

As they emerged from the trees, the villages and fields of Sparta appeared below. Everything looked so small from this height. All this was at stake if the Persian army descended upon them.

Lysander looked at his companion. His face burned with shame when he thought what Agesilaus had put them through. He put out a hand to stop Demaratos.

'Demaratos,' he began, 'what happened back there . . .'

'You were a hero,' said his companion. 'Don't feel ashamed of your Ordeal. And, don't worry, I have no intention of letting any of my friends know how much Agesilaus humiliated us. I'll have the glory instead, thanks very much! Anything else . . . well, can stay in the mountains.'

Lysander knew he and Demaratos had earned each other's respect – that much, at least, had happened over the past few days. But could Demaratos be trusted now that they were returning to the barracks? He'd find out soon enough.

'Come on,' said Lysander. 'We'd better hurry.'

They passed the vineyards and olive groves of the lower slopes. The Helot settlement lay further off. Timeon would be buried now, his family back at work, trying to put aside their loss. Lysander remembered the smoke rising from the villages by the sea, and imagined the Persians committing the same carnage here. The settlement, with its tightly packed houses, would burn quickly. Would Timeon's family soon be buried beside him? It was unthinkable. With Ares' blessing, the Spartan army would destroy any invaders, surely. But what if the Gods weren't listening? All Lysander knew was that they had to get back to Sparta – fast.

They made it to the main track into Sparta. Lysander had a stitch in his side, but was still trying to run. Demaratos jogged along beside him. Lysander could tell by the sheen of sweat that his companion was fighting the pain from the boar injury. A band of

Helots were making their way towards the village. Between them was a cart drawn by a donkey. It was laden with food – cheeses and olive jars – and stacks of firewood. Lysander's stomach growled.

The cart trundled to a halt as they approached and the men turned to look at them. Lysander realised that their unwashed bodies and grubby tunics made them look even poorer than Helots.

'Do you have any food for two travellers?' said Lysander, coming to a stop.

'This food is for the troops,' said a bearded man, sitting on the back of the cart. 'But I'm sure they won't miss a lump of cheese.' He used a small blade to cut two chunks, which he passed to Demaratos and Lysander.

'What troops do you speak of?' asked Demaratos.

The Helot looked at him as though he was mad.

'Have the Gods taken your senses, young one? All of Sparta is gearing for the attack. Where have you been?'

Lysander breathed a sigh of relief. A messenger must have got through from the south after all. Or perhaps Sparta had seen the smoke in the distance. It wasn't too late.

'We've been in the mountains for five days,' he said.

'In that case, fortune smiles on you,' said the man. 'You have been spared the preparations for war. Our masters have ordered all supplies to be brought to the centre of the villages. The army is gathering its strength to face the Persians.'

'The Persians are fools,' said Demaratos. 'No army has ever defeated Sparta.'

The Helots all laughed and Demaratos flushed. Lysander realised that they thought they were Helot boys.

'Let us hope you are right, young one,' said the bearded man. 'They say Vaumisa has ships filled with the strongest men of Persia, who carry swords so sharp that they can cut a man in half from scalp to bowels.'

'Who is Vaumisa?' asked Lysander. The name sounded exotic, and deadly.

The Helot patted the donkey's neck, and it began walking again. Lysander and Demaratos trailed behind.

'Vaumisa is the most powerful general of the Persian King, Cyrus. It was he who led the assaults on the Eastern Ionian provinces, defeating King Croesus and taking Miletos.'

Lysander had heard stories of the destruction waged upon distant lands, but they had always seemed so far away. By the time the reports reached Sparta they were as much myth as fact.

'But those lands are many days away,' he said.

'Vaumisa made slaves of the Greeks there. He set them to work stripping the forests and building a fleet of ships to carry his soldiers to Sparta.'

Demaratos laughed. 'The Athenians are cowards. A puff of wind would send them running. We'll show Cyrus that it takes more than one general and a few thousand men to challenge the might of Sparta.'

'You have a great deal of affection for the Spartans, boy,' said the Helot on the back of the cart. 'Maybe you should have your mother knit you a red cloak and you can pretend to be one.'

'Be careful how you mock the Spartans!' said Demaratos, placing a hand on the edge of the cart. 'You could be flogged to death for such impertinence.'

Lysander began to worry. He knew that Demaratos had Agesilaus' dagger in his sack. The Helot looked at his companions uneasily.

'I see no Spartans here. Do you?'

Lysander watched Demaratos's face for signs of anger, but there was only a sly smile.

'No,' said his friend eventually. 'I see no Spartans here.' Demaratos came to a stop and allowed the cart to pull ahead of him.

The two boys watched the Helots disappear round a turn in the road. Lysander breathed a sigh of relief. Maybe Demaratos really had changed.

As the barracks came into view Demaratos broke into an uneven run. The building that Lysander had once despised – with its cold dark walls and hard lessons – now looked like home. *I'll never complain about my bed of rushes again*, he promised himself. *And I'll never take another meal for granted*.

Lysander dashed through a side door into the dormitory, expecting to find his fellow students. The room was empty.

'Where is everyone?' asked Demaratos, throwing down his sack. The sound of voices came from outside.

They wandered into the training yard. All of the barracks students were standing in four neat rows, with Diokles pacing up and down. When Lysander saw the boys' red cloaks, he felt a rush of affection. These boys were his brothers in arms. It had taken him an Ordeal to realise this.

A few of the students looked over when Lysander and Demaratos came into the yard. Lysander heard someone whisper, 'They're back!'

Diokles turned to face them. His brow creased as he looked past them expectantly. *He's looking for Agesilaus*, Lysander realised. Diokles raised his eyebrows slightly, then turned back to the other boys.

'You are missing someone,' he said, without looking at them.

Lysander looked at Demaratos, who gave him a small nod. Lysander spoke loudly, so that everyone could hear.

'Agesilaus didn't make it through the Ordeal. He was torn apart by a pack of wolves.'

A gasp came from the assembled students. Diokles whipped round. He brought his face up close to Lysander's and seized him by the scruff of his tunic.

'You did nothing to help him?'

'There was nothing we could do,' said Lysander, meeting the tutor's gaze. 'By the time we approached it was all over.'

141

Lysander braced himself for a blow. But the tutor's face cracked into an ugly smile.

'I was Agesilaus' guide when he went through his own Ordeal. It seems I should have been tougher with him. You have passed the test, but let his death be a reminder that sterner challenges will come.' He turned to face the others. 'For now, let us congratulate the triumph of Demaratos and Lysander.'

The students let out a huge cheer and rushed forward. Lysander let them swarm around him. He peered through the crowd and spotted Orpheus, bringing up the rear as he hobbled over with his stick.

'Orpheus!' Lysander called over. 'How goes it?' A smile lit up his friend's face. Lysander had never been so pleased to see anyone. He pushed through the other boys to embrace his friend. They clung to each other, and Lysander realised that this was the first show of affection he had been given in days. Finally, Orpheus pulled away, wrinkling his nose.

'You need a bath,' he said.

'I need a meal and three days' sleep too,' said Lysander.

Leonidas waited behind Orpheus, shifting on his feet.

'What is it?' asked Lysander.

Leonidas came forward and held out his palm. The Fire of Ares lay coiled in the centre.

'Lysander, I don't know how to tell . . .'

'It's all right,' Lysander interrupted. 'I know about Timeon.'

Lysander took the Fire of Ares and read the inscription again. The letters were in an ancient language, but he knew what they said: *The Fire of Ares shall inflame the righteous.* 'Is that what I am?' muttered Lysander, remembering how he'd watched Agesilaus bleed to death.

Behind them, Demaratos had been hoisted on to his friends' shoulders and was being borne aloft around the exercise yard. 'What happened to your leg?' asked Prokles.

'I fought off a wild boar,' he was saying, 'but that was nothing compared to the wolf.'

'You fought a wolf?' said Ariston.

'You'll have to wait,' said Demaratos. 'I've hardly eaten for five days – I need some food.'

The boys crowded round Demaratos and begged him for details of the Ordeal.

'I can imagine surviving the wilderness for five days,' whispered Orpheus, 'but how did you live with Demaratos?'

Lysander laughed. 'It was hard at first,' he admitted, 'but we had bigger concerns. Without his friends to show off to, Demaratos isn't a bad person.'

Orpheus and Leonidas shared a look of amazement.

'Enough!' boomed Diokles. 'Lysander and Demaratos – clean yourselves and assemble in the mess. A meal awaits.'

★   ★   ★

Dressed in a fresh tunic, Lysander felt like a new person entering the dining hall. The boys were already lined up along the benches. The tables were laden with bread and steaming stew, but Lysander fought the urge to dig in.

'Fetch their cloaks,' said Diokles, 'so they can feel like true Spartans again.'

Demaratos's slave, Boas, brought his master's cloak, but no one brought Lysander's. Lysander rushed to get his own from the dormitory. Once, this would have been Timeon's job – but not any more. The thought made him remember the carving Hecuba had given to him. He took it from his sack.

Lysander retrieved his cloak from beside his bed and threw it over his back, feeling the familiar weight of the red cloth on his shoulders. He knotted it carefully, using Timeon's carving as a clasp. Then he turned back to the dining hall. At the doorway of the dorm, he paused and looked back at his bed, where Timeon had so often stood guard over him. 'I miss you,' Lysander whispered. Then he closed the door behind him.

Back in the dining hall, Lysander looked for a space to sit down. There was none.

'Over here!' Demaratos called. As Lysander made his way over, he could see the look of shock in Prokles' face. Prokles was one of Demaratos's close friends, and had always prided himself on being his favourite too.

'Make room for Lysander,' said Demaratos, shoving an elbow in Prokles' side.

Prokles spat a mouthful of half-chewed bread on to the table and stared at Demaratos in astonishment.

'You heard me,' said Demaratos. 'If Lysander is good enough to save my life in the mountains, he's good enough to share my table also.'

A murmur passed along the table, and Prokles shifted in his seat to give a place to Lysander. Orpheus was struggling to fight back his laughter. Ariston poured Lysander a cup of water. The gesture was small, but it meant everything. Lysander scooped out a bowl of the stew and ate greedily, hardly bothering to chew. They drank wine too, watered down in the way Spartan warriors took it. Lysander was on to his second helping of stew, and already a little light-headed, when Diokles stood up at the end of the table.

'Students, we welcome back Lysander and Demaratos from their Ordeal. They have proved themselves true Spartans.' The table raised their cups and cheered. 'Soon the rest of you will face the challenge too.' A second cry went up.

Diokles' face turned serious. 'You all know what is happening. War is on our threshold. Many of your fathers have already marched to face Vaumisa and his warriors. We must behave with dignity and honour while our soldiers defend Sparta. The Gods are on our side. We will drive the Persians into the seas from whence they came, and burn their ships before their eyes. We will spare no one, from their bravest warriors to their beasts of burden. For now, enjoy your meal.'

The table was filled with talk of war as the boys ate.

'You missed a grand sight, Demaratos,' said Ariston, slurping his stew. 'The army was mobilised the day after you left for the mountains.'

'Diokles was furious,' said Prokles.

Demaratos tore off a piece of bread from the loaf between them and dipped it in his bowl. 'Why?' he asked.

'Because he wanted to go too,' replied Prokles. 'But the barracks commanders have to stay. He's been sulking ever since.'

'We saw the Persian ships with our own eyes,' said Lysander.

'Don't be foolish,' said Ariston. 'How can you have seen them?'

'From the mountains,' said Lysander. 'We saw them burning the southern villages.'

Ariston sniggered. 'Are you sure you want this liar as your friend, Demaratos?'

'He's not lying,' said Demaratos. 'I saw them too.'

Ariston picked up his bowl and poured the remains of the stew into his mouth.

'Perhaps they were simply trading ships,' said Prokles.

'No, they were warships,' said Demaratos, banging his fist on the table. 'We saw archers on horseback.'

The table had fallen silent. Ariston and Prokles shared a look, and Meleager leant across.

'But how can you have?' he asked. 'The Persians are attacking from the north!'

'From the Arcadian coast,' added Ariston. 'That's where the army is marching to.'

But Lysander knew what he had seen.

'The whole army is heading north?'

'Yes,' said Prokles. No one was eating now.

A cold feeling swept over Lysander's skin. He stood quickly, knocking over his cup of wine. If the army were all marching northwards . . .

Lysander realised what this meant. The main invasion force was a diversion. Vaumisa would lead his raiding party from the south. Lysander ran towards the door.

'Where do you think . . .' shouted Diokles, but Lysander ignored him.

He had to get to Sarpedon's villa as soon as possible.

Sparta was defenceless.

CHAPTER 15

Lysander raced back through the outer village of Amikles towards his grandfather's house. The village streets were filled with people, but there was no disguising that the preparations weren't for market – they were for war. A cart passed, piled high with medical supplies: saws for amputations, stretchers and splints. Another carried firewood. An overseer paced between the buildings.

'Bring out all you can spare!' he shouted. 'All you can spare for the army. Your full larders will not keep the Persians at bay if our army is defeated.'

Lysander was running so fast, he almost skidded into a fat man carrying a pile of shallow trays. When he saw Lysander's red cloak, he gave an unsteady bow.

'Sorry, master, I didn't see you. I have to get these salted fish loaded up. All for our troops.'

Lysander hurried on.

Along the street, occupants carried out armfuls of whatever they had in their stores. Wood for burning, salted meat, jars of wine and medical supplies. Lysander had never seen Sparta mobilised in such a way. All the people were coming together in the face of the enemy.

Lysander passed the open front of a blacksmith's shop, where a hairy, bare-chested free-dweller was hammering out a molten red sword, his iron ringing out across the street. He saw the cloak on Lysander's back, and cried out to him.

'May the Gods be with you, Spartan. Don't be late for the battle.'

Lysander quickened his step and pushed his way through the crowds bustling in the central square of Amikles. The sight there made him stop. A huge mass of Spartan soldiers was gathered, drawn up in formation. Lysander counted at least twenty-five rows across, and perhaps the same number of columns. Nearly five hundred soldiers – a full battalion – all dressed in their uniform cloaks, with their shields slung back over their shoulders. Spear-tips glinted in the sun. A high clear voice lifted a song above all the other noise. The singer was a young man with dark skin – perhaps a slave from the city of Carthage over the Great Sea.

Many wealthy Spartans kept a foreign slave for entertainment, and the Carthaginians were reckoned the best singers. Lysander couldn't make out the words until he drew closer:

We praise those champions who lead the fight,
who give their lives in the front line.

149

In men who fear, all excellence is lost.
Cowardice is a fate worse than death.
Face the enemy, do not turn and run.
Nothing shames more than a wound in your back.

The song finished, and shrill pipes sounded from somewhere in the crowd. On the fourth blast, Lysander saw a Spartan soldier bring an instrument to his lips. Two other players followed suit, until all four were piping in unison. A horn sounded and a harsh cry echoed through the square.

'Spartans! We march to war! Come back with your shields, or upon them!'

Lysander watched as four soldiers moved out of the ranks to take the lead. Four more followed, and four after that, as the massed men narrowed into a column and began to file out of the square. All heading north to face the Persians. All heading away from Sparta when she needed them the most.

As Lysander hurried down the road to Sarpedon's grand villa, his cloak billowed out behind him. A convoy of dusty trailers rattled towards him. They were guided by a team of Helots streaked with dirt. A spear and other pieces of armour filled the carts.

'You're going the wrong way,' said Lysander to the lead Helot, as they drew alongside. He lifted his tired, hollow eyes.

'We've come from the battlefront,' he said wearily.

'How is the battle faring?' asked Lysander.

The slave shook his head.

'After a day's fighting, it is a stalemate. We drive them back with the phalanx, but the Persians regroup on the shoreline and attack again. Many have died – from both armies.' He waved his hand at the contents of the cart – Lysander looked closer. The armour and weapons were all damaged. Lysander saw a mud-streaked breastplate and a spear, splintered in two. There were several shields, bearing dents and spattered with blood. He swallowed, thinking of the men who must have died, their terrible wounds.

'Good day to you,' said the Helot, and pulled away, the rickety cart shaking along behind him.

Lysander continued to Sarpedon's villa. Two Spartan guards stood slouched either side of the gate. When they heard Lysander approach, they looked up and straightened their backs. Both were young men, perhaps twenty-five years old. Their cloaks were freshly dyed and their spears, by the looks of their straight and polished tips, had never seen use.

As Lysander headed between them, they lowered the shafts across one another, blocking his path.

'I need to speak with the Ephor Sarpedon,' said Lysander.

One of the soldiers smiled, and spoke to his fellow guard.

'Did you hear, Kyros, this boy has business with the great general.'

The other guard gave a snort, and leant forward.

'I heard, Alexandros. You're a little late for the Council, young one.'

'I am not here for the Council,' said Lysander. 'I'm here to see Sarpedon.'

The Spartan called Kyros lowered his spear point to Lysander's face.

'I'm telling you for the last time, boy. Sarpedon is in discussion with the other Elders. Be on your way.'

'Please, it is urgent. I have information about the Persian army.'

'And my grandfather was Achilles himself,' joked Alexandros. 'Now, move along,' his hand dropped to the hilt of his sword, 'or we can give you something more painful to think about.'

A slight figure appeared behind the two soldiers – dressed in a plain white dress.

Kassandra. It felt a lifetime ago that Lysander had left her behind as he walked towards the mountains.

'Let him in,' she ordered.

'But, my lady . . .' began Kyros.

'Do as I say,' interrupted Kassandra, 'or you'll answer to Sarpedon himself.'

The soldiers each gave a small bow and promptly uncrossed their spears. Lysander was admitted.

'Follow me,' said Kassandra. She led him along a corridor to the left of the entrance way, through a storage area piled with sacks, and into a bedchamber. Apart from a bed, there were several expensive-looking chests and the walls were hung with tapestries depicting the stories of the Gods. Her tortoise walked slowly across the tiled floor. An uncomfortable silence fell over the room and Kassandra couldn't meet Lysander's eyes. She plucked her pet off the floor and sat on the edge of the bed with it on her lap. Lysander remembered their strained words before he went into the mountains, and a feeling of guilt tugged at his conscience.

'Kassandra . . . I have to . . .'

'You are looking well,' she interrupted with a smile. 'You survived the Ordeal.'

'Yes,' said Lysander. 'I apologise for my behaviour before I left. You were right about Demaratos – we couldn't have survived without each other.'

'And he's safe too?' she asked. Lysander could hear she was trying to keep her voice under control.

'He's fine,' he said, 'but listen, I need you to help me speak with Grandfather. I have some important information.'

'Very well,' replied Kassandra. 'But he's talking with the other generals in the courtyard at the moment. We cannot interrupt.'

'I must speak with him right away,' said Lysander. 'It cannot wait.'

'It is a Council of War!' said Kassandra. 'They're meeting here to be away from prying eyes in the acropolis.'

'There must be some way we can sneak in,' said

Lysander. He spotted the door on the other side of the room and made for it.

'Don't be foolish, Lysander,' said Kassandra, putting the tortoise down, and trying to block the doorway. 'The Council values its privacy highly. Only the Elders are allowed to speak.'

Lysander had no choice – he could not waste a moment. He roughly pushed Kassandra aside and she cried out as she stumbled. But Lysander didn't look back; he slipped out of the room.

'Sarpedon will punish you,' Kassandra called after him.

Then he heard her give chase. *She is almost as stubborn as me*, he thought grimly. Lysander ran through a room lined with dining couches, emerging into a shaded outdoor area.

It was the courtyard where Lysander had trained with his grandfather. Only now it was thronged with red-cloaked Spartans, their backs turned to Lysander and his cousin. Many of their heads were bald, or grey-haired. The Council of Elders! The low murmur of urgent conversation filled the courtyard. Kassandra grabbed his arm and pulled him back behind a pillar.

'What do you think you're doing?' she whispered.

'I need to tell them what I've seen,' he hissed back. 'Persians, coming from the south.'

'You can't simply barge into a Council meeting,' said Kassandra. 'It's against the laws of Sparta – you'll get us both killed!'

Her words made Lysander stop. He needed to choose his moment carefully. The conversation suddenly stopped. He peered around the column and saw Sarpedon enter from a far door.

It was six days since his grandfather had wished him well in front of the barracks. Six days that had changed Lysander for ever.

'Elders of Sparta,' began Sarpedon, his voice filling the courtyard. 'My thanks for gathering here at short notice. News from the battle is good. The King who marches with the troops reports our army has withstood the Persian assault with courage. Many have fallen – at the last count over four thousand have died to protect the city. They will be able to walk in Hades with honour. Many more will die before the fight is won.'

As Lysander watched, another old man, with wiry muscles, stepped forward.

'Tellios, my fellow Ephor of Limnae,' said Sarpedon. 'Please say your piece.'

'Thank you, Sarpedon of Amikles,' replied Tellios. 'We trust your words, of course, but can we trust the army to triumph? A thousand armed Spartans will stay in the five villages to protect the King who remains here, but they are ready to take up their weapons and join the fight. We must send them to reinforce the bulk of the army.'

Another man turned to face the crowd.

'Fellow Councilmen, you know me as a man of

good judgment. I have faced the enemy with many of you by my side.'

'This is the truth, Myron, Ephor of Pitane,' said Sarpedon. 'Speak freely.'

'Then I will say that we should keep the final battalions in Sparta. Without them, we are defenceless. Even a small force – a few thousand Helots – could overwhelm us.'

'If the Persians break through, a thousand men will be useless,' protested the Ephor called Tellios. 'We must prevent that at all cost. The men should be dispatched immediately. The Helots will not revolt – they have as much to lose as noble Spartans. Anyway, after the punishment we meted out before, they wouldn't dare rise up again.'

The debate broke out amongst the men.

'How can you be sure, Myron?'

'The Helots are cowards – they have no leader.'

'The slaves are looking for their chance for revenge.'

'Silence!' called Sarpedon. 'We will have order in this Council!' The voices died down, and Sarpedon's face pronounced his fury. 'This is not the Assembly of Athens, where the mob shout over one another for attention. This is Sparta! We will have order.'

Lysander watched as the faces of the gathered men grew serious.

'We must put this to a vote. All in favour of keeping the garrison in Sparta, raise your hands.' Lysander counted the arms – twelve, including Sarpedon himself. 'All in favour of sending the remaining battalions north, show your choice.' Fourteen. 'So be it,' said Sarpedon. 'I will send a message to the King, telling him that the Council is decided: the remains of the army will head north immediately.'

'No!' Lysander shouted, stepping out from behind the pillar. He couldn't let the Spartans leave themselves defenceless. Kassandra looked at him, her face pale with fear. The grizzled faces of the Elders turned towards them, their faces full of suspicion.

'Spies!' said one of them.

CHAPTER 16

Four of the Elders ran towards him, sword-tips pointed straight at his neck. Lysander knew that if he moved, his life would be over.

'Don't hurt him!' shouted Kassandra. She pushed herself in front of him, regardless of the swords. The Spartans looked back hesitantly at Sarpedon, waiting for his orders.

'Kassandra?' came a voice. Sarpedon pushed between the armed men. His face was twisted with fury. 'Lower your weapons,' he growled, and pushed down the blade of the nearest sword.

He seized Lysander and Kassandra roughly by the arms, and marched them away.

'Wait,' said Lysander. 'I have information . . . about Vaumisa.'

Sarpedon let go of his granddaughter, and spun Lysander around, pushing him against a column.

'You have offended my household and the Spartan Council already. Don't try my patience with lies . . .'

'I'm not lying!' shouted Lysander, shaking his arm free. 'Persian ships have already landed on the south coast near Gytheion.'

The Council huddled in small groups and began whispering. One of the men looked over at Lysander and shook his head.

'The boy must be lying,' called Tellios, but Sarpedon raised a hand to silence him. 'Vaumisa wouldn't be so bold.'

'I saw them with my own eyes,' urged Lysander. 'Dozens of boats – the harbour villages were ablaze.'

'It cannot be,' mumbled Sarpedon, but he didn't sound convinced. 'The coastal villages would have sent word. They would have warned us.'

'They sent a messenger,' said Lysander. 'But the Persians already had men ashore. They killed him, with arrows.'

Sarpedon turned from him, and faced the anxious faces of the Council.

'It sounds as though he speaks the truth – the Persians are fond of their cowardly bows. It means they don't have to look into the eyes of the man they killed.'

Some of the men nodded. Tellios did not. He pointed at Lysander.

'How can we trust this boy? Look at him. He's not yet a man.'

'He is my grandson,' said Sarpedon, 'and he has completed the Ordeal. His word is as good as my own.'

Tellios bowed his head respectfully.

Sarpedon motioned to Kassandra. 'Leave us, grand-daughter.' Kassandra did as she was told, and Lysander turned to go after her.

'Not you,' said Sarpedon. 'Come with me.'

Lysander watched Kassandra slip into the villa, casting a last glance back in his direction. Perhaps he shouldn't have been so harsh with her earlier. Sarpedon strode back towards the centre of the courtyard. The crowd parted to let them through.

'We must make new plans,' bellowed Sarpedon.

What looked like a thick parchment lay rolled up on the ground. Sarpedon took hold of one end and pulled it open. Lysander saw that it was a cured animal hide. From its size, he guessed it belonged to a cow or ox. There were markings painted on the surface with brown dye. He recognised one word – Sparta.

'This map shows Sparta and the surrounding lands, Lysander,' said Sarpedon. He ran his finger over the markings. 'Here are the mountains – Taygetos to the west, Parnon to the east. The river Eurotas flows here.' He traced a line through the five villages to the sea. 'The Persian forces we know of have landed here, beyond the northern passes. We are holding them for now, but if they break through and reach the forests to the west, our advantage is lost. We must keep them in the open.' He looked at Lysander, his face hard. 'Show us, Lysander, where did you see the boats?'

Lysander studied the map, and laid his finger by the southern coast.

'And how many ships were there?' asked Myron.

Lysander thought back.

'At least thirty,' he said.

Sarpedon drew in a sharp breath. 'With a hundred men on board each ship, that makes at least three thousand. They'll be here at dawn.'

'We don't have enough men,' said Myron. 'They'll burn Sparta to the ground!'

Sarpedon stood to his full height and massaged his forehead with his scarred hand. Could three thousand Persians really lay waste to Sparta?

Tellios spoke next. 'We must evacuate the King to Taras, and send the city's treasures with him.'

'But what about the Helots?' asked Lysander.

Myron laughed. 'What of them, boy? They will burn in their houses or be taken for slaves. We cannot concern ourselves with their fate.'

'No,' said Sarpedon. 'The boy is right. We cannot abandon the city. If the Persians gain a stronghold, they will never be dislodged. They'll be like ants, swarming all over Greece.'

'And how will we face three thousand Persians?' asked Tellios, sneering. A few others murmured their assent.

'We'll gain nothing but more Spartan corpses for the birds to pick at,' said another.

A muscle in Sarpedon's jaw twitched as he listened to the other men.

'Better to live and fight another day,' said Tellios,

turning to the others. One or two nodded in agreement.

Sarpedon grabbed a pot, and flung it against a pillar. Earth and fragments of pottery exploded across the courtyard and Lysander flinched.

'You doubters bring shame on Sparta!' roared Sarpedon. 'You ask how we will face them? With courage! While we still have men, we still have hope. A thousand men await with their shields and spears, and every one of them is ready to give his blood! Which is more than can be said for you, Tellios!'

The crowd was silent. Tellios stared at Sarpedon. For a moment, Lysander thought a fight would erupt, but Tellios sat down slowly.

'You are living in a past age, Sarpedon,' he said quietly. 'This is a time to be practical, rather than shedding lives needlessly.'

'Tell us, Ephor,' said Myron. 'How will we repel the Persians?'

Sarpedon stared at the map, and then at Lysander.

'With an old wrestling technique,' he smiled. 'We will use a feint.'

Several of the Elders shook their heads, and Lysander heard someone mutter, 'He's weak in the head.' Lysander fought the urge to speak out. He knew his place.

Sarpedon knelt stiffly beside the map.

'Bring me some of those pebbles, Lysander,' he said, pointing to a pot. Lysander grabbed a handful and laid them on the map. Sarpedon positioned two lines along the mountain ranges either side of the river.

'We will send our one thousand Spartans in a pincer movement, five hundred on either flank along the tree-covered mountain ridges. We'll crush the Persians between them. Their armies will be in disarray.'

Lysander looked into Sarpedon's eyes. It was a brave plan, but risky.

'Vaumisa is no fool,' said Myron. 'Why would he fall for such a trick?'

'Because,' replied Sarpedon, lifting a finger, 'we will give him bait.'

The Elders exchanged glances, and Lysander heard hissed whispers. What was his grandfather planning?

'What will you use as bait?' he asked. Sarpedon glanced at Lysander, then looked quickly back at the map.

'We will need a battalion to meet the Persians on the plain,' said Sarpedon. 'To draw them forward. If Vaumisa scents an easy victory he won't be able to resist. I have fought his tribe before, many years ago. Many of you were with me in their land and saw the opulence in which they dwell, bedecked with jewels and gold. Persians are greedy. If they think Sparta is within their grasp, they will not hesitate.'

Myron the Ephor nodded.

'It might work,' he said, 'but where can we find another battalion? We'll need the remaining men on the flanks. We have no other soldiers.'

Sarpedon smiled. Lysander felt a pulse of excitement flow through him. *Is he planning what I think he's planning?* Lysander thought. *Could it be?*

'There are others who can fight,' Sarpedon said simply. Then he looked at Lysander a second time. Lysander understood immediately. His grandfather wanted him to fight for Sparta.

'Boys?' scoffed Tellios, coming to stand between the two of them. 'You want us to send students into battle against the ruthless armies of Persia? Has Zeus sent down a thunderbolt on to your head?'

'We can do it,' protested Lysander from behind Tellios. The older man turned round to gaze at him in open mockery. The crowd erupted into laughter, and Lysander's skin prickled with heat.

'Have any of you got a different plan?' he shouted. 'Or will you all scatter like a flock of starlings?'

One by one the men stopped laughing and straightened their backs. Lysander had deliberately stopped short of calling them cowards, but he could see he had their attention now.

'Sarpedon is right,' he said, walking around the courtyard. 'If we abandon it, the city will fall to Vaumisa, and all of Greece will hear that Spartans fled when they could have stayed to fight.'

'You should stay out of politics, boy,' said Tellios.

'This isn't about politics,' countered Lysander, spinning round. 'This is about being true to Sparta.' He found that his fist had come up over his heart.

164

'And what do you know of Sparta?' said Tellios. 'Before the summer, you were planting crops in the field.'

The crowd gasped at the insult.

'A Spartan would defend his name,' Sarpedon muttered from behind Lysander. Lysander knew what he meant – in the Council there could be no favours because of family. Lysander would have to prove his worth to these men. He turned back to Tellios.

'I can shoulder a weapon as well as any man in the phalanx,' he said.

'Can you, indeed?' said the Ephor. 'Then prove yourself.' He looked at one of the other Elders. 'Fetch those guards from the gate.'

The man looked at Sarpedon, as if asking permission. Sarpedon nodded.

Moments later, Kyros and Alexandros came into the courtyard, looking confused.

'You!' said Tellios, pointing to Kyros. 'Give the boy your sword.' Kyros unsheathed his blade and handed the hilt to Lysander. He took the weapon carefully, wondering what the Ephor had planned. He had only ever fought with the blunted weapons of the agoge. This was sharpened to a deadly edge. He looked at his grandfather, but Sarpedon's face gave nothing away.

'Right,' said Tellios, this time motioning to Alexandros. 'Let's see how well this boy handles a weapon. Fight him.'

'How will we decide who's won?' asked Lysander.

Tellios looked at Sarpedon, then at Alexandros, and finally at Lysander.

'Simple,' he said. 'The winner will be the one who's still alive.'

Alexandros drew his sword and came forward. Suddenly he didn't look like the idle soldier who had mocked Lysander at the gates. He looked like a soldier, intent on killing. Lysander held up his sword and swung it in an arc. Alexandros leapt forward, aiming at Lysander's chest. He parried downwards and spun away. Alexandros turned and came again, slicing at Lysander's head. Lysander ducked under the blow and came up, head-butting the Spartan under his nose, which exploded in a spatter of blood. Alexandros fell down with a cry of pain and dropped his sword, bringing both hands to his smashed nose. Lysander stood above the Spartan, his sword ready.

'Stop!' shouted Sarpedon. 'I'll have no more death in my home.'

An image of Lysander's mother flooded his brain. Breathing heavily, Lysander let his arms drop. He looked at Tellios.

'Now will you accept my word?' he asked.

Tellios' face was set in anger, but he gave a nod of his head. He looked at Kyros.

'Take your worthless friend away, and make sure all your barracks know that he lost to a boy.'

Kyros came forward and helped Alexandros to his feet. Trailing blood, they left the courtyard.

'Maybe Lysander's right,' said Myron, stroking his chin. 'If we do flee the city, the Persians might arm the Helots against us. That would make it impossible to regain control.'

'And the Athenians would laugh at us,' said another man.

'Enough talk,' said Sarpedon, addressing the gathering. 'It is time for action. Have your men assemble into two groups. Myron will command the eastern flank, Tellios that on the west. We will march before dawn, and meet Vaumisa's army on the plains south of Sparta. Death and honour.'

'Death and honour!' shouted the men, three times. On the third chorus, Lysander joined in. He had proved himself, but he knew the ultimate test was yet to come.

As the men left the villa, Sarpedon embraced each of them in turn, saying a few words. The atmosphere was grave and, when Lysander was alone with his grandfather, he saw that the older man was exhausted.

'Come here, my boy,' said the Ephor as he sat on a wooden bench. The map was still open in front of them, and Lysander walked around it until he stood before his grandfather.

'You were foolish to come here,' said Sarpedon. 'You could have been killed on the spot.'

'But I . . .'

'You were also very brave,' he interrupted. 'Like your father, Thorakis.'

Lysander saw tears flood his grandfather's eyes. 'Brave and foolish,' he repeated. 'It is not right for a son to die before his father, and even less for a grandson to meet death before an old man like me.' He stood up stiffly. 'But come, this is no time for sadness. I will send word to your barracks and others to assemble before dawn. Strabo!' he shouted. The slave scurried out. 'Take Lysander to a room and prepare him food.'

'Yes, master,' said the slave. 'Follow me, master Lysander.'

Lysander walked behind the slave, whose shoulders sagged. Strabo led him through a corridor and into a bedroom.

'This is the room . . .'

'. . . where Athenasia died,' said Strabo. 'It is the only one left. The Ephors are staying here tonight also. Better than sleeping outdoors, I'm sure.'

Lysander looked at the bed where his mother had spent her final days.

'Quite the Spartan now, aren't you?' said Strabo, leaning against the door frame and eyeing Lysander's cloak. All the obsequiousness he had shown Sarpedon only a few moments earlier had disappeared.

'Half my blood is still Helot,' replied Lysander.

'Ha!' sneered the slave. 'You proved where your loyalties rested when you stood with the Spartans against us on the night of the Festival. How many Helots perished because of your actions?'

'More would have died if your plot had succeeded,'

said Lysander, folding his arms.

'But not your friend, Timeon . . .' said Strabo, with a sly glint in his eye.

Lysander didn't know what to say. Strabo was right. Lysander sank back to sit on the bed, momentarily defeated.

'Anyway, when you meet him in the Underworld, you can offer your apologies.'

'What do you mean?'

'Well, surely you can see that death is close. Your boys' battalion will give time for the real soldiers to attack, but you will all be killed. Why do you think the old man looks so wretched?'

'Don't call him that,' said Lysander, bunching his fists.

'Careful, master, save your strength until tomorrow.' Then Strabo slipped away, leaving Lysander alone.

CHAPTER 17

Lysander dreamt that he was walking alone behind the cart that carried his mother's body. It was being pulled by Sarpedon's horse, Pegasus.

A voice broke the quiet, his mother's voice. It called to him: *Lysander, help me.* It came from among the folds of the shroud. *I'm still alive*, she whispered. *There's been a mistake, Lysander. Let me out of here.*

Lysander shouted for Pegasus to stop, but the horse didn't even flick his ears. His hooves stepped forward relentlessly. Ahead, the grave came into view – a gaping black hole, cut into the earth. He ran up, took hold of Pegasus' reins and yanked hard. The dark head didn't move. The black eyes were glassy. Lysander pulled again, but the horse's neck was like stone. He went back to the cart, and scrambled on board beside the body. He pulled at the linen covering his mother's face. It was tightly wrapped and he couldn't understand how she was able to breathe. But still her voice called to him. *Let me out, Lysander. I want to see you again. It's all a mistake.* As he pulled the layers away, he could make out features under the fragile linen: a nose, the hollows of her eyes. *That's right, Lysander. You're nearly there now.*

He pulled the final swathe aside. But it wasn't his mother. It was Timeon. Lysander fell backwards off the cart, crying out in terror.

'No!'

Lysander sat up in bed, panting for breath, his arms locked in front of him. The darkness in the room enveloped him.

A faint light appeared on the far wall. There were steps outside and a lantern appeared, illuminating Sarpedon's face. Strabo entered beside him, holding a bowl of steaming water.

'It is time,' said his grandfather.

Lysander threw off the bedclothes and washed quickly. With his sandals fastened, he gathered his cloak around him and left the chamber. Outside, a fine layer of condensation coated the columns around the villa's courtyard. Ice seemed to hang in the air, stinging his throat with each breath. A horse waited at the entrance way, grey clouds of hot breath rising from its nostrils.

'I prayed to the Gods for your safety in the mountains,' said Sarpedon. 'Now I will thank them for your return.' He paused for a moment. 'A messenger has brought word about Agesilaus' death.' Lysander couldn't tell if his grandfather was angry.

'There was nothing we could . . .'

171

'You owe me no explanations,' interrupted Sarpedon. 'The mountains are the test of a man, and you have made me proud. Prouder even than when my two sons returned.' Lysander pulled back his shoulders – he knew such words would not come lightly from his grandfather. 'Take my horse to the barracks,' said Sarpedon. 'Your comrades are waiting for you.'

'Where will you be?' asked Lysander.

'I wish I could join you,' said Sarpedon, 'but one Ephor must always remain in Sparta.' The moonlight caught a glint in Sarpedon's eye, and Lysander's grandfather gathered him in a tight embrace. 'You will need all the skills you have learnt, son of Thorakis. And remember, death is the greatest honour for a Spartan warrior.' Lysander seized the reins of the horse, and swung himself into the saddle.

'Death and honour!'

He kicked the horse's flank and galloped away from the villa. As he pounded through the bleak morning light, Lysander thought about Sarpedon's words. He'd said he was proud. Lysander was fired up with courage, though a part of him wondered if he'd ever see his grandfather again.

The sky was pale as Lysander tied up the horse outside the barracks. He ran inside. All the boys were fitting on their armour in the dormitory with the help of their slaves. Anxious faces turned to the door as he entered. Yesterday they had been boys talking about battles.

Now Lysander could see they knew that they were going to war.

'Lysander!' said Leonidas, rushing forward.

Demaratos lifted off his helmet. A clean bandage was tied to his leg, and he smiled in welcome. 'Sarpedon's hunchbacked messenger said you interrupted a Council meeting?'

Lysander nodded. 'News travels quickly.'

'And that you addressed the Ephors?' asked Leonidas.

Diokles marched into the room before Lysander could reply. He wore a dented breastplate over his chest, and a thick leather apron hung below. Both his forearms and shins were covered in armour. He carried a helmet under his arm.

'Hurry up, all of you,' he bellowed. 'Death does not like to be kept waiting.' His gaze fell on Lysander. 'Ah, the mothax has returned! Get on your kit immediately. Assemble outside.'

Diokles turned to leave. Then he looked back at a corner of the barracks and hissed, 'What in Hades are you doing?' Lysander looked over. There, by his bed, Orpheus was strapping a greave to his deformed leg.

'I'm coming too,' he said, not even looking at the tutor. 'Sparta needs every man able to fight.'

'Don't be foolish, boy,' spat Diokles. 'A cripple like you can't even stand straight to hold up a shield. You'd be no use in a shield wall. Stick to your music and singing.'

173

Orpheus pulled out his dagger, and hurled it through the air. It thudded into the wall a hand's breadth away from Diokles' face.

'The shield wall isn't everything,' said Orpheus. His voice was menacing – Lysander had never heard this from his friend before.

Diokles pulled the dagger from the wall, and walked slowly to Orpheus. Every boy watched in silence. Lysander's lame friend lifted his chin and stared straight back at his tutor. *Diokles is going to kill him,* thought Lysander. He edged forward, pulling his own sword from its sheath. But Diokles turned the blade in his hand, offering the hilt to Orpheus. His friend took the dagger back and sheathed it.

'Perhaps you can be useful,' admitted Diokles, before adding, 'But never do that again.' He turned to the roomful of boys. 'What are you all waiting for? Outside!'

Lysander darted to his chest, and pulled out the armour his grandfather had given him. He remembered the night of the Festival Games when Timeon had helped him fasten the pieces on. How long ago that seemed now. And how much had changed. The armour still sparkled from the last time Timeon had polished it. Around him, Helots helped the other boys climb into their armour, but Lysander struggled into his with no assistance. He placed a hand over the carving that rested against his chest.

'I can't bring you back,' he muttered, 'but I'll make you proud, Timeon.'

With the final arm-guard fastened, Lysander ran to the arms room and picked out a shield. Made of wood, it was coated in a layer of bronze, and marked with the Greek letter *L* to symbolise Lakedaimon, Sparta's ancient name. He slipped his hand between the two looped straps on the back and joined the lines of boys who waited in front of the barracks.

'Get to the front, Lysander,' shouted Diokles. 'You have completed the Ordeal.'

Lysander took his place beside Demaratos.

'Death and honour!' said his new friend.

'Death and honour!' Lysander replied.

As they walked towards Amikles, it felt like the day they'd set off towards the mountains. But this was no Ordeal. Lysander shifted his shield higher on to his arm. This was the ultimate test.

They fell into formation with four more sets of barracks students as they descended into the village. Lysander reckoned they were about five hundred strong now. They gathered at the stadium, the scene of Lysander's victory at the Festival Games. The parade ground was bustling with Helots, free-dwellers and red-cloaked Spartans. A few Spartans pushed through the crowd on horseback, barking orders. Mules were loaded with bags. Carts were piled with supplies. Sparks showered from a rotating grind-stone, where a barrel-chested man dripping with sweat held a soldier's sword to the spinning surface. A carpenter's mallet sounded out a regular beat.

'Put your shields in the baggage carts,' ordered Diokles. 'You'll need to save your strength.'

They trooped over and handed their shields to a Helot who stood on the cart, stacking them high and binding the stacks with rope. As he wandered back towards Diokles, Lysander noticed a small figure folding linen bandages on the edge of the parade ground. There was something about those small, pale hands . . . He approached slowly, watching the delicate fingers as they smoothed the linen. Lysander drew near and snatched back the cloak's hood.

'What are you doing here?' he asked.

'Be quiet,' hissed Kassandra, pulling the hood back over her head. 'You'll draw attention to me.'

'You haven't answered my question. What do you think you're doing? Women don't fight for Sparta, and certainly not the granddaughter of an Ephor.'

'I'm not going to join the army,' said Kassandra. She pointed to a Helot talking with a soldier a few paces away. 'I've bribed that Helot to take me with the baggage.'

Lysander shook his head. He would have to put a stop to it.

'Does Sarpedon know?' he asked.

'Of course not,' said Kassandra. 'You must promise me that you won't tell him.'

'But you might be killed,' Lysander protested.

'That is so,' said Kassandra, 'but why should all the

176

glory belong to men? I can be useful, too. Maybe I can't hold a spear, or take a place in the phalanx, but there are other ways. Perhaps I can help the physicians deal with injured soldiers, or take new weapons to the front line . . . Besides –' her tone was accusing, 'at least I won't be ignored this way, or treated like a maidservant.'

'I'm sorry I pushed you aside at the villa,' said Lysander. Kassandra looked unmoved and lifted her chin in defiance. 'But your grandfather will never forgive you if you do this.'

'By the time he finds out that I've not ridden to Thalamae with the other wealthy women, it'll be too late to do anything about it,' she said.

'Please, go back,' Lysander began, but Diokles appeared at his side.

'There isn't time for gossip now. Leave these Helots to do their jobs.'

'Promise me you'll reconsider,' said Lysander.

'Enough!' bellowed Diokles.

Kassandra looked at Lysander from under her hood, and he could see the fear in her face. *She's terrified*, he thought. *And too proud to admit it.* With a last imploring look, he mouthed, 'Go home.' Then he was pulled away.

The boys stepped out in unison, marching four abreast. Free-dwellers had gathered along the side of the track, and scattered petals at their feet. Some shouted words of encouragement.

'May the Gods bless you!'

'Drive the Persians into the sea!'

Others offered sacrifices at smoking altars at the roadside, burning barley, or pouring wine into the earth. The boys marched past the graveyard where Lysander's mother and father were buried, and he offered a silent prayer to Hades, God of the Underworld: *Let them smile upon my deeds.*

Low murmurs of excitement passed down the line.

'How many do you think there'll be?' said Hilarion in the row behind Lysander.

'The commanders estimate almost three thousand,' said Leonidas.

'Do you think they'll give this battle a name one day?' asked Prokles.

'The Battle of the Southern Plains, perhaps,' said Ariston.

'Or the Battle for Sparta,' said Demaratos.

'We'll be able to tell our grandchildren that we fought,' said Prokles.

'If we live that long,' said Hilarion, laughing nervously.

Diokles rode in silence beside them, his face betraying no emotion. The crowds stretched all the way to where the road crossed the river on its journey south, but began to thin out after that.

As they marched away from Sparta with the river beside them, Lysander looked around at his fellow students. Even with their armour, with real weapons that could kill, they were still only boys. What awaited them at the end of this march? And how many of them would return to Sparta alive?

CHAPTER 18

They had been marching for most of the day, following the churned, muddy tracks of the main battalions who had gone before them. The green of the mountain forests on either side had leached to grey and the moon rose above them, a pale spectre on the horizon. Demaratos seemed to be walking well once again. Lysander's own toes stung where the blisters had formed and burst and formed again, and his face was crusted with sweat that had dried on his skin.

They rounded a bend in the river, and the sight made him think of the depths of the Underworld. The camp was huge. On both sides of the river, scattered fires blazed under the dusk sky, and flaming ashes rose above, caught on the breeze. The shadows of men huddled around the edges, or lay on their shields. An orange glow illuminated grim profiles.

'Break ranks and make camp here,' ordered Diokles, the weariness telling in his voice.

A group of Helots unyoked the baggage carts that

had accompanied them, and led the beasts of burden towards the water to drink. Lysander and his comrades unloaded the firewood and provisions. While they built their fire, two pigs were lifted from the back of the cart, their stumpy legs squirming in the Helots' arms. Both panicked when they saw the slaughter knife, but their squeals were cut short by a blade into the jugular, their blood collected in bowls as an offering to the Gods.

Lysander and others saw to the lighting of the fire while the animals were gutted and the carcasses cleaned at the water's edge. Lysander's nostrils soon caught the sweet scent of roasting meat.

A Spartan soldier strode over to their area. His long hair was pale brown and tied back, showing a mass of scar tissue where his left ear should have been. His skin looked tough, like leather, and his face was heavily lined, with a cleft in his chin. Only his eyes looked lively and alert.

'I am Septon. Who is the leader here?' he asked.

Diokles stood up some distance away and faced him.

'I am. What news?'

The soldier came forward and sat on his haunches by the fire, gesturing for Diokles to join him.

'Do you have any wine for a weary messenger? I'm thirsty.'

'Lysander,' said Diokles. 'Bring some wine for our guest.'

Lysander dashed to a cart and seized one of the wine

flasks and a bowl. As he returned, the two men were already talking, seated opposite each other as the fire-light played over their faces. The boys nearest their fire, including Leonidas, were all listening. Lysander handed the flask and drinking bowl to Diokles, and sat down in earshot.

'The Persians have moved in from the shoreline,' said Septon, 'and have forded the river. They occupy the breadth of the plain, and have somewhere near four thousand men.'

'Four?' said Diokles, pouring wine into a shallow bowl. 'We were told three.'

'They have been reinforced,' said the soldier, adding a little water to the wine. 'We have sent a raiding party of three hundred men, in the hope of causing some havoc amongst their lines. It's a risk, to send away that many of our number. But perhaps the Persians will be put off a fight.'

'Very good,' said Diokles, offering the two-handled bowl to the other Spartan. 'But let's hope there are some Persians left for us.'

'Indeed,' said the soldier. He took a deep draught, and wiped his mouth with his sleeve. 'The main battalion will split into two before dawn and take to the hills on either side. You will draw up your troops at first light and send them into battle down the centre of the plain. The Persians will think they are facing only a small contingent and come at them hard. With the Gods on our side, this will buy us enough time to swoop in from the flanks and crush them.'

'It sounds like a suicide mission,' said Diokles, smiling broadly.

The soldier slapped the tutor hard on the back, and straightened up.

'What more could a Spartan ask for?'

Lysander shared a look with Leonidas, who was warming his feet by the fire's edge. He gave a wan smile. Lysander hoped the fear wasn't so obvious in his own eyes.

Thankfully, it was a dry night. After they had all eaten their fill, some of the boys had drifted asleep on the cold earth, huddled together for warmth. Lysander decided to take a tour of the camp. He threaded between the campfires, taking care not to tread on any dozing soldiers. The men were indistinguishable beneath their red cloaks, and in the gloom Lysander couldn't tell if he was looking at boys or men. He found himself moving through the Helot area, where men slept beside their animals. He couldn't see Kassandra anywhere. Hopefully she'd seen sense and gone back to her grandfather's villa.

He couldn't help thinking how different his life would have been, if his father had really been a Messenian. He too might be sleeping here amongst the servants, depending on the Spartan army for his survival. But Lysander's father was Thorakis, a brave warrior. How many times had he been on campaign, lying beneath the stars and waiting for the day of battle to dawn? He touched the pendant at his chest, feeling his father's spirit flow through him. He would need the Fire of Ares when the fighting came. He prayed to the God of War: *Keep my shield firm and my spear straight*.

Suddenly there were shouts in the distance. Lysander heard the word 'Help!' echo across the camp, and other words he couldn't make out. They became louder and more urgent. Lysander heard 'water' and 'physician'. Something about the man's cries made Lysander break into a run. Panic filled his heart as he recognised the cry of terror. Across the camp, figures were waking and climbing to their feet.

Lysander reached the man first.

He stumbled out of the darkness, his red cloak half torn away. Under the starlight, his face was pale. 'Help,' he muttered again, almost in a whisper, and toppled forward. Lysander caught him, and struggled under the Spartan's weight. The soldier's arms sagged over his shoulders, his nails digging into Lysander's back.

'Let me help you,' said Lysander, lowering the soldier to the ground. His hand touched something slimy and wet under the man's cloak. It felt like raw meat.

'Please . . . some water,' whispered the man, his voice rasping as blood bubbled out of his mouth. His hands released their grasp on Lysander, and he fell limply to the ground. Torchlight flickered across the soldier's glazed eyes. Gingerly, Lysander pulled aside the remains

184

of the dead soldier's cloak. The Spartan's side was a bloody mess, lacerated from what looked like an axe wound. Lysander could see the man's glistening intestines bulging out through splintered, pale ribs. Other Spartans gathered around him. He pulled the cloak back to cover the sight.

'It's the raiding party,' said one. 'They've returned!'

Lysander saw other figures approaching through the darkness. They weren't in any sort of formation. Some walked alone, others supported each other, unable to stand on their own. A horse lumbered into the camp, dragging something from a stirrup. It was a leg. Two arrows protruded from the horse's hindquarters.

Many were gathering now from the camp, bringing torches, blankets and water. An injured soldier stepped into view. The side of his face was black with dried blood, and the eye was missing where the socket had been smashed.

'Where is Septon?' he asked. 'Where is the commander?'

'I am here, Thyestes,' replied the general. In the darkness, the deep lines of his face seemed carved in stone. 'How do you fare?'

'I am still alive,' said the Spartan called Thyestes. 'Though I'm a Cyclops now.'

Septon smiled grimly. 'Come, take a seat by the fire, comrade. Tell me what happened?'

Lysander hovered by the edge of the flames as Thyestes spoke.

185

'We reached their camp in the darkness, and all was quiet. We thought to have caught them unawares. I burst into the first tent, but there was no one inside. My fellow soldiers found the same. All the tents were empty. It was a trap.' He stopped and wheezed for breath, clutching his side. 'As we readied to leave, they surrounded us, demanded our surrender. I told them that Spartans do not surrender. Their arrows came thick as hail. We are all that's left of three hundred men.'

Septon nodded grimly. 'Rest, for now,' he said, and nodded to Lysander. 'This boy will find you some food. We fight again at dawn.'

While the other wounded soldiers were tended to, Lysander brought Thyestes water to bathe his face, and some meat and bread. They spoke quietly while the others slept.

'What is your name, boy?' he asked, cutting a chunk of pork away with his dagger.

'Lysander.'

'And who is your father, Lysander?' asked Thyestes, chewing slowly.

'His name was Thorakis,' he replied. 'I never met him.'

Thyestes stopped eating and took a drink from his flask. 'I only know one Thorakis – son of the current Ephor Sarpedon. But he had no children.'

'My mother was a Helot,' said Lysander. He couldn't help the note of challenge in his voice. 'Sarpedon is my grandfather.'

Thyestes drew a deep breath. 'So you're a mothax, a half-breed?'

'What of it?' said Lysander, feeling his anger flare.

'It's no matter,' said Thyestes. 'If a man can hold a shield and a spear, and face death without flinching, he is a man whatever his birth. Thorakis was brave – you should be proud.'

'I am,' said Lysander. 'Did you know my father?'

'We were in the same barracks for many years,' said Thyestes. 'Thorakis had a strong spear arm and the heart of ten men – I will be with him soon, I think.' The Spartan winced as a coughing fit racked his body, then spat out a mouthful of bloody sputum on to the ground.

'You must see a physician,' said Lysander. 'You're in pain.'

Thyestes laughed softly.

'There are different sorts of pain, Lysander. I'd rather have these injuries than have failed to do my duty. Go to sleep now. Tomorrow will be hard.'

Thyestes settled as best he could for sleep. Lysander walked the short distance back to his own fire, and lay down beside Demaratos.

'Are you all right?' asked his friend.

'I'm fine,' said Lysander. 'Go back to sleep.'

But as he pulled his cloak around his shoulders, the Spartan's words echoed in his mind. There different sorts of pain. Perhaps that of the body was the easiest to deal with. He remembered Hecuba tearing at her hair and beating her chest in sorrow. He remembered Timeon's blood on his face.

Injuries got better. Grief, and guilt, took longer to heal.

'Wake up, Lysander,' said a voice in his ear. It was Demaratos. 'The flanking battalions are leaving. We must gather in front of the camp.'

Lysander stood up and stretched. Demaratos had already moved on to wake the next boy. The fire had died completely, and Lysander had to stamp his feet several times to warm himself. A small way away, Lysander could see Thyestes was still asleep on his side, so Lysander walked over and knelt beside him.

'Wake up,' he said, shaking the man's shoulder. Thyestes' body rolled slowly towards him. His lips were blue and a fly buzzed lazily over the gore of his face wound. Thyestes' hand still clutched his dagger. Lysander felt for a pulse in the soldier's wrist, but he knew already that the Spartan was dead. The skin was icy and the arm stiff with rigor mortis.

'Give my greeting to my father,' he whispered, and closed Thyestes' remaining eye.

Lysander peeled Thyestes' fingers away from the hilt of his dagger, and untied the sheath from his belt. He strapped it to the side of his lower leg above his sandal. The dead Spartan wouldn't need it now.

All over the camp, boys were fixing on their armour. Lysander found his soldier's outfit on the cart and positioned each piece with care. The bronze was cold against his skin, but reassuring. The vambraces would allow his forearms to deflect glancing blows, and the greaves would protect his lower legs. The heavy pieces of leather that hung from his waist wouldn't stop a direct spear thrust, but they would prevent wayward strikes from drawing blood. He helped Leonidas to fasten his breastplate and the prince fastened Lysander's. The lion's head depicted on its surface fired Lysander with courage. He noticed that Leonidas's hands were shaking.

'They've been doing that since I woke up,' said Leonidas.

Lysander slapped him on the shoulder.

'Only a fool scorns death,' he said. 'After today, no one will call you a coward again.'

Leonidas's hands steadied a little. He slapped Lysander back.

'Will you stand beside me in the phalanx?' he said.

'I'd be honoured,' Lysander replied.

With his short sword hanging at his side, he fastened his cloak again. The boys were lining up to collect their spears from the back of a cart. Lysander and Leonidas joined the queue. Diokles marched amongst them, banging his shield with the hilt of his sword.

'Phalanx formations!'

The time had come. Lysander curled his fingers around the shaft of his spear. It was slightly taller than his head. The iron tip was a point more than a handspan long. At the bottom end was the lizard sticker – a lump of bronze with a shallow point, blunted and heavy. Not for stabbing, but for smashing into the faces of men on the ground. Lysander hoisted the spear above his head to test the balance, then joined the others. Orpheus stood towards the rear.

'I can't run with the forward ranks,' he said. 'But I'll be right behind you.'

'Let's hope the Gods are still on your side,' said Lysander.

Lysander looked at his friends. They'd been there for him since the first day in the agoge.

'I want to tell you, if I don't . . . if I'm killed . . .'

'You don't have to say,' said Leonidas. 'We all feel the same.'

He put his hand out in a fist, as Agesilaus had done before they went into the mountains. Orpheus followed suit. Lysander didn't hesitate and placed his on top.

The boys had gathered in ten rows, each roughly fifty soldiers long. Lysander and Leonidas pushed to the front. Demaratos was already there, and they took their places beside him. With his shield on his left arm, he would be able to protect Leonidas. Demaratos on his right would protect him. All eyes were fixed ahead, where a dark line stretched over the horizon.

The Persians were coming.

As the enemy ranks inched forward, Lysander could make out helmeted heads. Sunlight glinted off their weapons – long curved swords and battle-axes. Their shields weren't round like his own. They were tall oblongs, stretching from the shoulder to below the knee. The Persian line halted some two hundred paces away. *One of us will have to give way*, thought Lysander, *and it's not going to be us.*

Diokles emerged on horseback in front of Lysander and the other troops. He trotted along the ranks, moving boys backwards so that the line was straight. Then he drew up in front of the phalanx.

'The phalanx relies on order, courage and trust. The boy to your right will defend you. You will defend the boy to your left. Stay tight. Stay firm. Every time you gave your blood and sweat in the agoge was to prepare you for this moment. This is what you were born for.' He pointed with his sword across the battlefield. 'These are your enemies now. I will not lie to you. We are outnumbered. Many of you will not see the sun fall this evening.' Behind Lysander a boy whimpered. Diokles ignored him and continued. 'If this is to be your last day with the living, make it a glorious one. Lift your shields high. Hold your spears firm. If you give your life, do not give it lightly. Make Vaumisa know how hard a Spartan dies. Death and honour!'

'Death and honour!' shouted Lysander and his comrades.

'Start the drums!' ordered Diokles.

Behind the line, a heavy beat sounded across the plain.

191

Boom!
Boom!
Boom!

'March!' barked the tutor.

Lysander's row stepped forward in time with the beat. His stomach churned and his legs threatened to give way. He concentrated on keeping his shield level and covering Leonidas's right side. That was the only way the phalanx would succeed. Somewhere behind him another boy whimpered, and the bitter smell of urine wafted under his nose. Lysander's whole world was the narrow view from his helmet. The drumbeat quickened. He gripped his spear more tightly, and broke into a jog. The ground thundered. The Persians stayed still. *Why don't they come?* thought Lysander. He could see that their helmets were conical, some with spikes on top. A cloud of dark smoke rose quickly above the Persian line. It took him a moment to realise what it was.

'Arrows!' shouted Leonidas, his voice muffled through his helmet.

He was right. The curtain of shafts floated, rising in an arc towards them.

'Ignore them!' shouted Diokles from his horse. 'Maintain order!'

The arrows left Lysander's field of vision over the brim of his helmet. He started to run. Then there was a sound like wind gusting past his ear. A thud sounded to his right. Prokles screamed and fell. Then thuds all around, sounding like hail on the roof of the barracks. Cries of terror rose to the skies. Another boy filled the place beside him. The drums speeded up again. They were running now and boys were shouting war cries above the drums: 'Death to the Persians!' Still the Persians were steady in their ranks. Lysander didn't know how many of his comrades had fallen. *More glory for those who remain.* He pushed on.

The Persians were no more than fifty paces away now. Had the drums stopped? He didn't know. They were all running now, and Lysander lusted for Persian blood. The shield on his arm weighed nothing. The spear in his hand was an extension of his body. Lysander saw a Persian, with his sword raised above his head. Lysander could make out the wicker of his shield, the white of his eyes under painted lashes. *You're mine*, thought Lysander.

'Ready your spears,' ordered Diokles. Lysander adjusted his grip, as he had done so many times in training. The others in the line did the same. The shouts around him grew to a crescendo as they reached ten paces' distance from the Persians, closing still. Lysander found himself joining in with the cries.

'For Sparta!'

CHAPTER 19

The Persian's shield buckled under Lysander's spear, and the point hit the middle of his chest. Lysander felt resistance for a fraction of a heartbeat before the tip buried itself in the flesh. Even if he'd wanted to stop, Lysander couldn't have. With the weight of the phalanx behind him, he crashed through the front rows of Persians, pressing the shaft further through his victim until they were almost face-to-face. Warm blood sprayed across Lysander's cheek, and the Persian's face twisted in pain. His eyes rolled back in his head, and Lysander felt the warmth of his final breath as it escaped in a sigh.

Lysander brought his foot up to the Persian's chest and pushed him off the spear, leaving a trail of blood along its length. The whole of the enemy front line had been pushed back, and the Spartan phalanx had held firm.

'Crush them!' came an order from behind.

Lysander pulled his shield back into position, and the

194

row straightened. It was the Persians' turn to charge. Their line ran forward. Lysander knew what to do. Just before they hit, he took a step forward. Shields and weapons crashed together along the line. The sound was deafening. The line held.

Lysander adjusted his grip for an overarm thrust and marched forward with the others. Leonidas gave a blood-curdling cry at his side. The enemy were already edging backwards. There were shouts from their lines too, in a language that Lysander couldn't understand. It seemed their commander was telling them to stay and fight. Lysander came within range and aimed at another Persian ahead and lunged with his spear. The tip only grazed the Persian's neck. His enemy saw his chance and lunged with his sword towards Lysander's armpit.

'No!' It was Demaratos. He pushed out his shield and the blade clattered safely away from Lysander. Lysander stabbed again with his spear and this time it pierced the Persian's throat. He gave a stifled cry. Lysander forced the point downwards, into the chest cavity. The Persian dropped his sword and shield, fell to his knees and reached up to his torn neck. Blood gushed over his fingers as he writhed on the floor.

The phalanx pushed on. With the Persians on the back foot, everything depended upon Lysander and his comrades holding the line, and using their spears. A mass of dead and dying Persians lay at his feet. Groans of agony filled the air. He trampled over the fallen men as the line surged on. The Persians were looking unsure now, and some were even beginning to turn. The enemy commanders issued angry shouts.

Lysander felt a sharp pain and fell to one knee, crying out in surprise. A bloodied Persian had rammed his dagger into the back of his calf. Lysander lifted his spear and rammed the lizard-sticker down on to the Persian's arm. He saw the limb buckle as the bone shattered. The soldier screamed and writhed on the ground. The other Spartans surged around Lysander, continuing their advance. He lifted the spear-butt and struck again, this time into the Persian's face. The Persian's head twisted and he stopped moving.

Lysander pulled the dagger from his leg. It was bleeding, but not heavily. He struggled to his feet and hobbled on. He was in the middle of the Spartan ranks now, and could see the front line lunging with their spears ahead. Then he saw Hilarion. He was lying on his back, looking upwards, gripping his side with bloody hands. His chest rose and fell quickly as he gasped for breath.

'Leave him!' came a voice from behind. It was Diokles. 'You're here to fight!'

Lysander threw himself forward once more, picking his way over the tangle of bodies. Most were Persians, but a few red cloaks were scattered among them as well. Lysander recognised some of the faces from his own barracks. Each one tightened the knot of his anger. He saw a gap and charged back into the fray with an underarm thrust that lifted a Persian off his feet as the spear entered his groin. Lysander pulled it loose, then drove it into his chest, twisting the point deeper.

A cheer rose through the ranks, and Lysander looked up to see the remaining Persians turn away. It seemed like they were running for their lives. Lysander turned to the boys around him. Their faces, mostly covered in blood, were ecstatic. Could victory be so easy?

'Let's go after them!' said an older boy. Lysander felt people pushing from behind. Another voice called out, 'We can finish them off!' and another, 'Glory will be ours!'

Lysander heard Diokles' voice, faint under the clamour, 'Hold your lines!' but if anyone else heard, they didn't listen. Lysander found himself forced aside and knocked to the ground as the rows behind streamed past in pursuit of the retreating Persians. The phalanx fell apart.

'No!' shouted Diokles.

'Are you all right?' said Leonidas, helping Lysander to his feet.

'Yes, but . . .'

Ahead, the Persians were still running back towards their commanders, but Lysander could see something wasn't right. The retreat was *too* orderly. When they were thirty paces away, with scattered Spartans hotly in pursuit, the Persians began to fan out. Their line thinned as it became wider, stretching out across the plain.

'What are they doing?' shouted Leonidas.

The tips of the Persian line suddenly turned right around and started charging back towards the Spartans. It was no retreat, it was a tactical move, and his comrades were running right into the middle of it.

'They'll surround us!' shouted Lysander. A few of the Spartans stopped and turned at Lysander's cry. 'It's a trap!' he yelled. 'Pull back!'

More of the pursuing Spartans had obviously seen the threat as well. The advancing body split into groups to face the Persian attackers now threatening to encircle them.

'The shield wall will be useless,' said Leonidas. 'We have to help!'

'Fall back! Fall back!' Diokles was shouting. The Persians were coming at the boys from the sides and the front. Lysander saw Demaratos desperately plunge his spear into the stomach of an attacker. While he was trying to free it another Persian came from the side, raising his mace, thick with spikes.

Lysander didn't think. He hoisted his spear and threw it, extending his arm to make sure it flew straight. The Persian was swinging his mace towards Demaratos's neck when the spear-point caught him in the ribcage. The tip exploded through the other side of his body, sending the Persian staggering sideways, and dumping him on to the ground. Demaratos tugged his own spear out of the fallen man's flesh, and shot Lysander a nod of thanks.

'Where are the reinforcements?' said Leonidas, glancing around. 'They should be here by now.' Lysander scanned the slopes to the east and west. Only rocks and trees. The battalions were nowhere to be seen.

Isolated Persians were edging around the rear of the Spartan troops. Diokles charged his horse through a group of the enemy, scattering them. One managed to grab his reins and Lysander saw his tutor slip from the saddle into the mess of bodies. He darted forward to help.

'I'm coming,' he shouted. But a solitary Persian rounded to face Lysander and grinned, showing teeth filed to points. Lysander kept running, dropped to a crouch, and lifted his shield to block the Persian's scimitar. He swung his own sword. The blade sliced into his enemy's leg and lodged against the thigh-bone. The Persian screamed. Lysander pulled out the sword, shoved the Persian back with his shield, and swung again at the neck. The head flew off in an arc and the corpse coiled to the floor.

A body crashed into Lysander, sending him sprawling to the ground. Ariston. Blood bubbled from between his lips as he mouthed a silent prayer – half a spear was protruding from his back. Lysander eased Ariston's body off himself. A Persian stood above them, holding the other half of the spear. Lysander kicked him in the shin. The Persian bent over. The distraction was enough. Lysander swung his sword, slicing through his enemy's

199

cheek and sending him spinning to the ground. But the Persian was still alive, and turned slowly, his mouth open in a bloody roar of pain. Lysander scrambled over, lifting his shield. The Persian's eyes were wide with astonishment as Lysander rammed the rim down hard across the neck, killing him instantly.

Lysander climbed to his feet, feeling every muscle in his body fired with power, tears of anger and fear streaming down his cheeks. He wanted to throw himself back into the fight, to kill again or be killed. The battle raged; around him were the sounds of metal on metal, of death-cries and swords slicing into flesh, of terror and pain. Diokles was up and hacking at a figure on the ground, who was desperately trying to protect himself as the blade's edge cut him to pieces. All around, Persians and Spartans mixed in a crowd of slaughter – it was impossible to tell which side was winning. Lysander pulled his shield up, seized his sword and plunged amongst them. He found Orpheus, bravely facing two Persians. He moved just as he had on the training ground – ducking below their scimitars and fending off blows with his shield and sword.

'I'll show you the taste of iron,' Lysander shouted. One of the Persians turned to deal with him, thrusting at his face. Lysander dodged to the side, feeling the edge of the blade nick his helmet. He hacked down hard at the Persian's shoulder, severing his arm. It clattered to the ground, still holding the sword.

But the Persian didn't give up, and kicked Lysander

fiercely in the stomach, knocking the wind out of him, before grabbing the sword from his own severed hand. Blood poured down his side as he came forward, swinging the blade in dizzying arcs. Lysander straightened and stood his ground.

'Come on, you Persian dog!' he screamed. 'I'll show you how a Spartan fights.'

The Persian brought his sword down from above and Lysander blocked with his shield. He drove his own blade into the Persian's belly. The soldier let out a pitiful cry and toppled backwards.

Lysander pulled out the sword and the Persian squirmed on the ground. A few paces away, Orpheus swung his sword at the Persian in front of him with a grunt. A thin red line appeared across his throat. Blood overflowed the gash and drained down his front. Orpheus finished the job with a stab to the heart. He turned to Lysander; his eyes were wild and his armour covered in blood.

'This is nothing like the training in the barracks,' he said.

There was a flash of metal, and Orpheus's face twisted as he looked down. A small, two-headed axe was buried in his leg. A Persian, heavily armoured in an unusual suit of linked metal pieces, stepped close. He was carrying a second axe. He brought the handle down on Orpheus's helmeted head, and Lysander's friend crumpled to the ground. Lysander ran towards him.

'Get away from him!'

The Persian was reaching down to pull his other axe from Orpheus's leg, when Lysander's sword struck his arm. The blade didn't pierce the armour, and sent shockwaves through Lysander's shoulder. He swung again, this time at the head. The Persian moved forward at the same time, under the blow and burying his shoulder into Lysander's stomach. Lysander was lifted off the ground, and thrown through the air. His sword slipped from his fingers as he smashed back on to the earth.

The soldier trudged forward, knelt on Lysander's chest and landed a heavy blow to the side of his helmet with the axe. The Persian aimed another blow, but Lysander managed to lift his arm and deflect it with his elbow. He was losing strength. His opponent swung again, and Lysander felt the axe bite into the top of his arm. He couldn't help the cry that escaped his lips. His enemy lifted the axe above his head, the blade dripping blood.

Lysander closed his eyes and prepared for death.

CHAPTER 20

But the blow never came. Lysander dared to open his eyes. The axe hung loosely from the Persian's hand. A spear-tip pushed out through his mouth and his tongue squirmed around the wood. The body shivered, and the Persian sank sideways.

Diokles stood above him, breathing heavily. The lower part of his helmet had been torn away, leaving a jagged edge. His eye patch had come off as well. He offered a hand to Lysander, who took it and jumped to his feet.

'Thank you,' he said. 'You saved my life.'

'I saved a Spartan,' said Diokles.

Lysander retrieved his sword and looked around. The Persians' superior numbers were beginning to tell. Spartans were falling everywhere, their torn red cloaks littering the ground. He couldn't see Demaratos, Orpheus or Leonidas. Another block of Persians was coming over the plain towards them.

'We're losing the fight,' said Diokles. 'We'll have

to fall back.'

'No!' said Lysander. 'We can't. The Persians will have a clear road to Sparta. We have to hold them until the reinforcements arrive.'

Two arrows hit Diokles in the chest. He stumbled towards Lysander, holding out his hands. Lysander caught him, but could only slow the fall. Diokles grunted as he hit the ground. Almost immediately, blood welled in his mouth. He held on to the back of Lysander's neck, his brow creased in pain.

'Not a bad way to die,' choked his tutor, straining to keep his head raised.

'Let me get help,' said Lysander.

'There's no help for me now,' he gasped. His head sank back on to the ground, his lips moving slowly. Lysander leant closer to hear his words. They came in a whisper.

'You've made a good soldier, mothax.'

The grip behind Lysander's head relaxed. Diokles was dead.

Lysander pulled his tutor's cloak over his body and stood up. All the times Diokles had bullied him weren't important now. On the battlefield he had proved himself a comrade. Lysander saw the Spartan forces were being pushed back towards their own camp. Two Persians ran at Lysander, each wielding a curved scimitar. Anger burned through his limbs.

Drawing his sword, he darted left, so that one Persian blocked the other's path. It was a trick he'd learnt in the one–against–many fights from the barracks. To deal with one opponent at a time. The Persian swung his sword, and Lysander sidestepped. The blade whistled past his ear and slid down his shield.

With his enemy exposed, he sliced upwards with the point of his own sword into the soldier's unprotected armpit. The Persian tried to lift his own sword again, then looked in horror as he understood. His arm was hanging by a torn section of muscle and his blood sprayed down his side from the severed artery. Lysander lunged at his companion, but he was a skilled swordsman, parrying Lysander's blow.

The Persian brought his sword down in an arc. Lysander buckled his legs, pushed his shield on to the blow, then twisted full circle in a crouch to gain maximum power. His sword cut a horizontal arc, slicing the Persian's leg clean off. The Persian crumpled, and screamed in agony.

'You can die slowly,' shouted Lysander, already walking away.

Lysander scanned the area where Orpheus had been fighting, but he couldn't see his friend anywhere. 'Orpheus?' he shouted. 'Where are you?'

A moan came from the sea of bodies ahead, and an injured Persian lifted his arm. Lysander edged nearer and saw that the Persian was dead, with half his head missing and shards of skull buried in a deep wound. There was a Spartan beneath him.

'Orpheus?'

Another groan. Lysander ran forward and pushed the dead Persian off his friend. Orpheus was lying on his side, his face pale. His leg was hanging off at an angle and soaking the ground red. Lysander knew his friend would die if the blood flow wasn't staunched soon.

'Hold on,' he said. While the fight raged around him and shouts in Persian and Greek filled the air, Lysander used his sword to tear off a strip of Orpheus's cloak. He carefully threaded it above the bleeding stump, then tied a knot. Orpheus hissed through his teeth as Lysander pulled the tourniquet as tight as he could. The bleeding slowed instantly.

The main fight had moved beyond them, as the Persians pushed the remainder of the army back. Lysander took in the corpses of Persians and Spartans that lay strewn around him, some still moving feebly or groaning in despair. Where were the flanking reinforcements? If they didn't come soon, the battle would be lost completely.

'Go back to the fight,' said Orpheus. 'Leave me here.'

Lysander ignored his friend's protests, and put his arm around Orpheus's shoulder, lifting him to his feet. The Persians and Spartans were fighting among the baggage carts now, and the cries of fear came from the Helots. Lysander could see them cowering beneath some of the carts. Others had seized whatever weapons came to hand and were joining the fight. They were hopelessly outmatched, and Lysander longed to go to their aid. But he couldn't leave his friend. He watched with despair as a middle-aged Helot, holding a charred log as a club, ran at a Persian soldier. The warrior stepped aside and ran his sword across the Helot's stomach, drawing a chilling howl from his lips.

A horn sounded. Lysander glanced around, scanning the battlefield. Then he saw. On the steep slopes either side of the plain, red-cloaked men were emerging. They edged from among the trees, their spears bristling. Hundreds of Spartan soldiers. He turned back to Orpheus.

'The flanking battalions! They're here!'

The horn sounded again, and the waves of soldiers poured down the slopes. The effect on the Persians was instant. Many peeled away from the fight with the Helots and the remaining Spartan boys, and began making for the sides of the plain. They roared a battle cry as they charged to face the new attackers.

Lysander continued back towards the baggage carts. Suddenly he heard the pounding of hooves from behind. He dived to the side, taking Orpheus with him, as a troop of gleaming white horses thundered past.

The band was led by a Persian rider covered in golden armour, brilliant in the sun. Ten others, dressed entirely in black, galloped at his side.

It had to be Vaumisa.

A group of three Spartans charged at the Persians. The black-clad bodyguards formed a tight wall with their horses. Two unshouldered their bows and, in a single fluid movement, unleashed arrows into the Spartans' chests. The third Spartan looked on, unsure what to do, before charging at the horses with his spear. The nearest Persian reared on his horse, then brought its hooves down on him.

Vaumisa twisted in his saddle, barking orders, but the bulk of his troops seemed in chaos as the Spartans came at them from the slopes on either side of the plain. They had formed hastily into two ranks, one facing east and one west, to meet the latest assault. The remainder continued to fight the Spartan boys beside the supply area. Lysander lifted Orpheus and began guiding him back towards a safe area of the camp.

'You have to stay and fight,' said Orpheus.

The Spartans from the hills crashed into the Persians from both sides, splintering shields and raising screams of terror and pain from the enemy. Vaumisa turned his horse, and signalled to his bodyguards. They charged among the baggage carts and Lysander lost sight of them. Where were they going? A few dozen Spartans remained in the supply area, driving back the Persians who were still there. Lysander saw a Persian collapse into the ashes of one of the fires, writhing on the ground with a spear in his stomach. Over the fallen enemy stood Leonidas. When his eyes caught Lysander's, he ran over. Close up, Lysander could see a gash extended across his forehead. Blood and sweat slicked his face, but he looked jubilant. He whooped and slapped Lysander on the back. When he saw

Orpheus's wound, he blanched.

'Your leg . . .'

'I'm lucky; it's my bad one,' said his friend with a thin smile.

Lysander turned to Leonidas.

'Vaumisa and his bodyguards are here.'

'Here?' said the prince. 'In the camp?'

Lysander was nodding when a high-pitched scream rang out above the other sounds of the battlefield. A figure ran through the ashes of a dead fire fifty paces away, leaping over the corpse Leonidas has speared. Lysander recognised the grey cloak with its distinctive black hood.

'Kassandra!' he shouted.

Behind her appeared Vaumisa on horseback, his golden armour reflecting the sunlight. His bodyguards rode behind him in a V formation. Kassandra tripped over a rock. Vaumisa bore down closer. For a terrible moment, Lysander thought she'd be trampled beneath the hooves of his steed.

'Look after Orpheus,' he said to Leonidas, throwing down his shield. He couldn't afford to be slowed down. The prince took Orpheus's weight and Lysander sprinted towards Kassandra, drawing his sword.

As Vaumisa closed in, and Kassandra struggled to her feet, the Persian leant from his saddle with an outstretched arm. His hand held no weapon.

'Kassandra!' Lysander shouted again. He could see he was too late. Vaumisa seized Kassandra by the top of her cloak and threw her across his saddle. His cousin squirmed and kicked against her captor as Lysander stood before Vaumisa's stallion, brandishing his sword.

'Leave her alone!' shouted Lysander.

Vaumisa drew up in his saddle. His bodyguards fell in beside him. Lysander ran forward. He wouldn't allow them to take Kassandra.

One of the archers levelled his bow and drew back the string. The jagged tip was pointing directly at his chest. Lysander slowed. He couldn't dodge an arrow.

'Halt, Spartan!' boomed Vaumisa. He was a huge man, with a tanned face and large, deep-set eyes. The black shadow of a beard clouded his jaw and cheeks. His armour seemed to be made up of hundreds of golden scales, interlapping over his massive frame. Without his shield, Lysander knew he had no chance. He stood in front of the Persian general. The bowman's hand was steady and he looked at Lysander without pity.

'You are brave, Spartan,' said Vaumisa in a strange accent, 'but you'll learn that there is more than bravery to being a soldier.'

'Like kidnapping innocent girls?' Lysander said.

Vaumisa laughed. 'Don't try my patience. Be grateful that I am giving you your life today. Move aside, and enjoy the years ahead.'

The Persian's laughter was too much for Lysander.

'I'm a Spartan, and I'm not afraid to die!' he said.

The smile fell from Vaumisa's face.

'Very well.' He nodded to the archer. 'Kill him.'

Lysander felt the arrow hit him, like a vicious punch to the chest. The force made him spin around and he fell to the ground, landing on his face. He couldn't move. The sound of horses' hooves receded into the distance. He struggled to breathe. *Am I dying?* he wondered. *Is this what it feels like?*

'Lysander?' came a familiar voice. 'Lysander! No . . . no . . . no!' It was Leonidas.

'Is he dead?' joined in Demaratos.

Lysander wanted to speak, to tell them that he wasn't dead, but he still hadn't caught his breath. The pain in his chest was overwhelming. A hand tugged at his shoulder, and pulled him on to his back. Lysander opened his eyes. Two silhouettes were moving above him. His two friends.

'Wh—?' Lysander's hands moved over his chest, expecting to find blood. His fingers touched the arrow shaft. No pain.

'Huh!' Demaratos laughed. 'Look! The arrow hit that clasp.'

Lysander looked down his body and saw that Demaratos was right. The pain in his chest was gone. The arrow tip was buried in the wood of Timeon's carving. He sat up. Demaratos seized the carving in one hand and the arrow in his other and gave a tug. The shaft came away, but the arrowhead remained lodged.

'The Gods must be smiling on you,' said Demaratos.

CHAPTER 21

'Kassandra is here?' said Demaratos, his face uncomprehending.

'She sneaked along with the baggage handlers,' said Lysander. 'She wanted to play her part in the war for Sparta.'

'Why didn't you tell me?' said Demaratos, grabbing Lysander's arm. 'You know what she means to me!'

'I thought I'd persuaded her not to,' said Lysander, shaking him off. 'We haven't got time to waste. They headed back towards the sea. On horseback. I'll go after them, you have to go back to Sparta and tell Sarpedon.'

'I'm coming with you,' said Demaratos. 'You can't take on Vaumisa on your own.'

'I'll take a message to the Ephor,' said Leonidas. 'Take that horse.' He pointed to the edge of the battlefield, near to where a well-drilled line of Spartans were seeing off a small group of Persians. A horse stood with its head bowed. A Persian archer with only half his scalp attached hung limply from the side, tangled in his stirrups.

Demaratos ran over to the horse and Lysander followed him. Together they pulled the dead rider off and climbed into the saddle, Lysander at the front.

'May the Fates look on you kindly,' said Leonidas. Lysander kicked the horse's side and galloped up the edge of the battlefield, heading south.

The stallion was strong. Lysander steered him up the slope on the eastern side of the plain, down which the flanking army had advanced. Once on the ridge above, they had a view of the whole battlefield. The tide had well and truly turned and the fight was dying out. Though a few Persians were still resisting, small pockets had given themselves up, and were throwing down their weapons. The ones who were fleeing were being picked off with spears to the back. Not a brave way to die.

The tracks left by Vaumisa and his retreating band of horses could be clearly made out in the mud.

'Hang on,' said Lysander as he drove the stallion in pursuit, leaping over small bushes and fallen trees. His arms ached from gripping the reins so tightly, and he could feel Demaratos's arms around his chest like hoops of iron.

'Slow down!' he yelled. 'You'll get us killed!'

'I can't,' Lysander yelled back. 'We have to catch Vaumisa. It looks as though they're heading to the coast

– perhaps a ship is moored there.'

They entered a thicket of trees, and the thin branches whipped at his face. He steered through the trees.

'Duck!' he shouted as a low branch scythed towards them. He felt it brush his hair as they passed.

Emerging on the other side, the sea sparkled in the sun. Lysander saw a group of white horses, their heads bowed and munching grass. Something was wrong. Where were the riders? Then he understood: ahead, the ground dropped away, plummeting down to the sea in a sheer cliff face.

Lysander yanked hard on the reins, and the horse snorted, rearing on its hind legs. Its hooves skidded across the ground in a cloud of dust and it toppled backwards, throwing Lysander to the ground. He landed on top of Demaratos, who let out a cry. Thankfully the horse crashed beside rather than on top of them. The stallion struggled to its feet and galloped off into the forest.

Demaratos stood up and pointed down to the sea.

'Look!' he said.

A small cove the shape of a horseshoe nestled between two rocky headlands. The shoreline was mostly made up of large boulders, with a few spots of sand. On one of these, Vaumisa and his bodyguards were climbing into a small boat that knocked against the rocks. Kassandra stood between two Persians, each gripping an arm. She struggled between them, but was powerless. They dragged her across the sand and into the shallow water, then threw her roughly into the boat. Four rowers manning two oars were seated in the middle of the craft. Once they were all aboard, with Kassandra flanked by two bodyguards, one of the crew pushed the boat out of the shallows with his oar and rejoined the others. In time, they heaved away from the shore. The faint splash of oars reached Lysander's ears.

'They can't be going all the way across the sea in that,' he said. 'There must be a larger boat beyond the peninsula. Come on, we have to get down there.'

Demaratos nodded, and began to take off his armour. Lysander did the same – there was no way they could complete the treacherous descent laden down. A steep path, shielded by rough gorse, weaved down the cliff face. The earth between the rocks was soft and sandy, and pebbles clattered at every step.

They picked their way down as quickly as possible. By the time they reached the base of the cliff, Lysander's legs were shaking with the effort and the rowing boat was a speck rounding the headland. From here they could see a larger ship, bristling with oars, anchored a short way from the cliffs.

'How can we get there?' said Demaratos. 'They can row quicker than we can swim.'

'The boat is anchored close to the headland. If we can get to the tip, maybe we can climb down.'

Demaratos looked unsure.

'Do you have a better plan?' said Lysander.

216

Demaratos shrugged and shook his head. 'Let's go!'

Lysander led the way over the slippery rocks, limping from one to the next, taking care not to let his feet fall through the cracks. Demaratos was close behind, breathing heavily. White foam churned beneath the boulders, sending up occasional sprays of salty water that stung his many grazes and cuts from the battlefield. They reached the headland at the end of the rocky patch and Lysander was grateful to have his feet on dry land again. The headland was little more than a narrow tongue of land covered in low scrub. It rose as it entered the water, ending in a steep, snub-nosed cliff where a Persian ship stood at anchor.

They ran up the slope until they reached the end of the headland. The sight of the Persian vessel close up made Lysander draw a gasp.

The ship was a bireme, with two tiers of oars, locked at ease above the water. It stood bow on to them in the water, the stern pointing out to sea. A single mast stood in the centre, with a wooden structure – the forecastle – built forward of the mast and overlooking the deck. Crewmen swarmed over the vessel, too busy to notice Lysander and Demaratos watching them, and the sail was being hoisted. Lysander guessed the ship would be under way as soon as the anchor was pulled up and secured. He could see the other Persian ships at anchor further out, waiting for their warrior crews to return.

Some thirty feet below, waves crashed into the base of the cliff. The water swirled with dark and forbidding eddies. Lysander unhooked his cloak and pulled off his sandals. All he wore was his tunic, still filthy from the battle. His only weapon was the dagger strapped to his leg.

'There could be rocks beneath the surface,' said Demaratos, peeling off his own cloak.

'What choice do we have?' answered Lysander. 'We can't let Vaumisa take Kassandra! After three?'

Demaratos nodded. Lysander edged towards the drop. The sunlight sparkled on the dark water below.

'One . . . two . . . *three*!' He pushed himself off and leapt into the void. For a moment, he felt weightless in the air, but then the pull of gravity made his stomach lurch into his mouth. The air whipped past his ears and the swirling water rushed towards him. Lysander hit the waves feet first. It filled his nostrils and forced his eyes open. The cold seemed to seize upon his heart and squeeze. The air burst from his lungs in a rush of bubbles.

Which way was up? He hung in the water until the bubbles thinned, desperate for breath. He was aware of Demaratos, suspended in the water beside him. His friend began kicking in the water, and Lysander swam after him. His chest was tight and his lungs were close to bursting. His heartbeat pounded in his ears. He heaved upwards with powerful strokes.

Lysander's head broke the surface of the water. Demaratos was choking beside him, coughing up sea water. Lysander drew deep breaths that made his chest burn. He slowly recovered enough to take stock. They were several feet from the bottom of the cliff, and the waves rolled beneath them, lifting them gently up and down. With Demaratos, he swam to where a black rock jutted from the water and clung to its side. It was the only hiding place they had in this vast ocean. Four boat-lengths away, the enemy ship rocked in the water. He could see movement in the lower deck as the oarsmen took their seats. Someone was shouting orders. A figure appeared at the front of the boat, standing over the anchor pulley.

'Quick,' said Demaratos. 'They're preparing to depart.'

'We've got to be careful,' said Lysander. 'If the soldier sees us, it's over.'

Another order was barked, and the lower set of oars lifted in unison, before splashing into the water. The boat crept back to loosen the anchor from the seabed, and the figure on the prow began to wind in the rope, bending deeply at the waist as he heaved. The wooden pulley creaked. Lysander dived underwater and set off in a breaststroke towards the ship, ploughing onwards with all his strength. He was beyond exhaustion. His arms felt like iron as he dragged himself through the water. When he needed to take a breath, he came up to the surface as slowly as possible, sucked in a lungful of air, and dived again.

The third time he came up, they were approaching level with the prow, hidden from the oarsmen on the port and starboard sides. Demaratos was beside him, and Lysander put a finger to his own lips. If they made too much noise, the Persians might still be alerted. All would be lost. The ship's hull loomed out of the water above him. He rested a hand against the rough wood, which was covered in a slimy green weed.

'There's no way we can get up,' he whispered to Demaratos, who was treading water beside him.

'Yes, there is,' replied his friend. 'The anchor rope.'

Why hadn't he thought of that? The rope was still emerging from the water, dripping with water and seaweed. It was as thick as his arm, made of interwoven fibres. Lysander pushed off the hull and caught it with both hands. It was slippery and he twisted in an effort to hold on. He had to wrap his legs around the rope as well to prevent himself sliding off. Gradually, as the pulley creaked above, Lysander felt himself lifted out of the water. Demaratos grabbed hold of the rope too. Lysander prayed that the Persian at the pulley wouldn't feel the extra weight.

When the brim of the deck approached, he reached out. He released the rope and swung his other hand over. He pulled himself up so that he could peer over the deck.

The massive bare-chested man who had been pulling up the anchor locked the wheel and walked along the deck beside the forecastle, disappearing around the corner.

'Quickly!' hissed Demaratos, beside Lysander now.

Lysander heaved himself up on to his elbows, and raised a leg on to the deck. Demaratos scrambled up beside him. The planks felt warm against his skin as he lay on the deck, panting. They were aboard.

Close up, the forecastle looked like a small wooden hut built on the deck. Against the back of it leant a simple ladder – a plank with grooves cut in either side. The forecastle shielded them from the view of the rest of the ship. Sounds of guttural conversation were drifting from the bow end, and there was a heavy thud of feet on the deck.

There was a splash as the oars entered the water again on one side, and the stern shifted a few degrees.

'We're turning around . . .' whispered Demaratos.

Lysander pointed to the ladder. *Shall we look?* he mouthed. Demaratos nodded.

Lysander went first, carefully placing his feet on the rungs. The ladder creaked a little, but the sound mingled with the other noises on the ship. They found themselves on a raised platform, boxed in by a low guardrail of polished wood. The ship had turned a full half circle, so the prow now faced out to sea. On his belly, Lysander crawled to look over the edge.

He drew a breath. Below them, standing on the deck, was Vaumisa. He was a giant. *He must be three times my weight*, thought Lysander. A slave with skin as black as ebony was helping him to remove the outer pieces of scaled armour. The bodyguards, still wearing their black leather, were staring back towards the shore. They had removed their helmets, revealing heads shaved bare.

Demaratos tugged at his shoulder, and stabbed a finger to the left side of the deck. Kassandra was crouched among two huge coils of rope. Her hands were tied behind her back and her mouth was gagged. Two red streaks marked her cheeks.

Below them, Vaumisa was now washing his muscular arms and thick neck, scooping water from a bowl held by the slave.

Lysander slipped the dagger silently from its sheath on his leg.

'What are you doing?' hissed Demaratos.

'Stay out of sight,' replied Lysander. He clenched the cold blade beneath his teeth. The autumn sun was warming his skin, but still goose pimples broke out over his flesh. Lysander could smell the sweat from the general's skin. He would only have one chance, and if he failed, they'd all be dead.

Lysander leapt off the platform towards Vaumisa.

CHAPTER 22

Lysander hit the deck. He thrust both hands in Vaumisa's chest, sending him flying on to the deck. Vaumisa's face registered panic. Lysander swung a fist into his stomach, feeling the muscles tighten in his enemy's abdomen. The general bent double, wheezing for breath. Several of his bodyguards charged across the deck, but Lysander was too quick for them. He seized Vaumisa's long hair with his left hand, and the dagger with his right. He tugged back on the Persian's dark locks, and rammed a knee into the back of his legs. Vaumisa crumpled as Lysander brought the blade against his neck.

The bodyguards stopped dead.

For a few breaths, everything was silent. Kassandra's eyes were wide. Beneath the tip of his dagger, Lysander could see Vaumisa's pulse beating rapidly in his throat. He tugged back harder on the hair and pressed the tip of the blade into the flesh. Vaumisa drew a breath through his teeth as a bead of blood trickled towards his chest.

One of the Persian soldiers broke from the crowd and came at Lysander, sword in hand. Lysander backed away, keeping his grip on Vaumisa, but the soldier raised the sword above his head. Kassandra gave a muffled scream.

Suddenly the Persian was thrown back through the air, and landed hard against the railings on the side of the vessel. There was an arrow sticking out of his chest. The dying man looked down at his wound in astonishment, then stared above Lysander's head. Demaratos was standing on the platform, already stringing a second arrow and bringing it to bear on the other Persians. He gazed down the shaft.

'Get back,' he shouted. 'All of you.'

He must have found a bow and arrow up there! Lysander thought.

Demaratos's intention was clear. The Persians backed away.

Lysander's breathing had steadied, and his fingers ached around the hilt of the knife.

'Is there anyone here who understands Greek?' he shouted across the deck.

Vaumisa shifted a little on his knees.

'I need no translator, boy,' he spat. 'What is it you want? You will have it, then I'll throw you overboard. If the fish can stomach your Spartan flesh.'

Lysander nodded towards the bodyguards.

'First tell them to throw their weapons on the deck.'

Vaumisa barked an order at his men. They looked at each other uncertainly. Vaumisa repeated the order, and one by one, the Persians unsheathed their swords and threw them down.

'Now what is your pleasure, *master*,' said Vaumisa sarcastically.

'Release the girl,' said Lysander. Hope filled Kassandra's eyes.

'She is my prize,' said Vaumisa.

'She's just a Helot,' he said.

Vaumisa laughed. 'I know well what she is, boy. And I also know that two Spartans wouldn't risk their lives for a slave.'

'Release her,' said Lysander, ignoring Vaumisa's taunts, 'or the deck will be soaked in the blood of a Persian general.'

Vaumisa hesitated, then shouted an order in Persian, and one of his men hurried forward and untied Kassandra's ropes. As soon as her hands were free she rubbed her wrists and climbed to her feet. She walked towards where Vaumisa knelt on the deck. She spat in his face.

'Thank you, Lysander,' she said.

Vaumisa wiped the spittle away with his arm, and smiled up at Lysander.

'And what now, brave Spartan? How will you make your escape? You cannot kill us all, and you cannot swim away.'

Lysander looked up at Demaratos unsurely. His comrade still stood with his bowstring taut and an arrow trained on the deck below.

'We can take Vaumisa's boat,' Kassandra said.

The general laughed.

'And what will prevent me chasing you down,' he said, 'or my archers from cutting you to pieces with arrows?'

'Because,' said Kassandra, 'you'll be coming with us. Lower the boat.'

Vaumisa's face fell. He shouted an order, and there was a scuffle below deck, as some of the oarsmen moved about.

'You think you have beaten Vaumisa,' said the general to Lysander and Kassandra. 'But you will both die slowly for this.'

'Tell that to the Spartan Council,' said Lysander.

Vaumisa shouted another order.

'Tell them to move more quickly,' Lysander said. Kassandra's head jerked up.

'Look out!' she shouted. Lysander looked up, as the bare-chested Persian who had pulled up the anchor appeared on the forecastle and barrelled into Demaratos from behind. The arrow zipped from his bow and darted harmlessly into the water. At the same moment, Lysander heard a noise beside him and turned. Another rower, wearing a loincloth, swung an oar towards his head. His neck jarred painfully. Then nothing.

Water splashed over Lysander's face. He tasted blood inside his mouth and he could feel that one of his teeth was loose. He was sitting up on a hard surface. Opening his eyes, he squinted. The sun was impossibly bright and all he could see was the deck at his feet. *You fool!* he cursed himself. The boat was just a distraction: Vaumisa must have kept him talking while his men below planned a trap.

Lysander couldn't move his hands. They were tied and the rope was already chafing against his skin. He was tied to someone else.

'Demaratos?'

'You're awake,' replied his friend behind him.

Lysander's head was heavy and thudded with pain.

'Is Kassandra safe?'

'I'm here, too,' she said. Lysander turned his head slowly. The three of them were tied around the central mast of the ship.

'We were stupid,' said Demaratos. 'Vaumisa wasn't ordering his men to lower the boat. He was organising a trap.'

'You *were* stupid,' said Vaumisa as his shadow fell over them. 'But what can one expect from a Spartan? I've heard your people cannot even read!'

'The Athenians spread those rumours,' said Demaratos. 'They are only jealous because they cannot hold a spear.'

Vaumisa laughed, but the smile quickly faded.

'So tell me, Spartan,' he said, kicking Lysander on the bruise over his broken ribs. Lysander moaned as the pain brought him close to blacking out. 'Why did you risk everything for this girl?'

Lysander grimaced.

'Curse you,' he said.

'Come,' said Vaumisa. 'Satisfy my curiosity. I will make your death a quick one.'

Lysander remained silent.

'They're my protectors,' said Kassandra.

Vaumisa raised an eyebrow. 'Are they indeed? I would expect Sarpedon's granddaughter to make better choices.'

Lysander's pulse quickened.

'I wasn't sure at first,' said Vaumisa. 'My men simply wanted a hostage. When you shouted her name on the battlefield, I couldn't believe my luck. But there's really no mistaking it, is there?' He stroked the side of Kassandra's face. 'You can see it in the profile – this girl is no Helot.'

One of the bodyguards came to Vaumisa's side, and whispered in his ear. The general shook his head and spoke a few words, before turning to Lysander and his friends.

'Cleeto wants to know if it's time to sail home,' he nodded to the Persian beside him, who came forward brandishing a knife, 'but I've told him that plans have changed.'

Cleeto knelt beside them on the deck. Lysander avoided looking into the Persian's eyes. If he was going to be their executioner, Lysander didn't want to give him the pleasure of showing any fear. Lysander heard the blade sawing on a rope. Were they being freed? He tried to move his hands, but they were still tied. Demaratos stood up, a look of uncertainty playing on his features. *Why are they only freeing him?* Lysander wondered.

'Why have the cub of the wolf,' said Vaumisa, 'when one can have the head of the pack? I have dreamt about vengeance for so long. I thought I could take Sparta by force, but now I can do so by guile. You!' he pointed at Demaratos. 'You can obviously swim. Head back to the shore. Tell Sarpedon that I have his beloved Kassandra, the daughter of Demokrates. He must be here by nightfall, or I will peel the skin from her body before she dies.'

Demaratos didn't move.

'No!' said Lysander, pulling at his bonds again. 'Don't do it!'

'Go now!' ordered Vaumisa, drawing his sword. 'Every moment you waste her death draws closer.'

Demaratos looked at Kassandra and Lysander.

'I'll come back with help,' he said. He turned, and took four strides to the edge of the deck. Then he jumped over the side. With a splash, Demaratos was gone.

Lysander watched anxiously as the sun sank across the sky, turning the water to gold. Would Sarpedon come? If he didn't, they were dead for sure. But if he did, what good could come of it?

On the deck, the Persians brought out huge legs of lamb, spiced breads and flasks of wine and began feasting. They sang strange, repetitive songs. Every so often, one of them would cast a look at Lysander and Kassandra, and curse in angry Persian. Vaumisa seemed on edge, pacing the deck and looking back towards the shore.

'Do you think Sarpedon will come?' whispered Kassandra.

'I hope not,' said Lysander. 'Vaumisa has won, whatever happens now. Better that the two of us die, than we risk the life of Sarpedon.'

'This is all my fault,' she said quietly.

Cleeto was looking at Lysander. He tried to avoid the bodyguard's eyes, but each time he looked up, they were upon him. Finally, the Persian stood up and walked over, chewing a piece of bread. When he reached Kassandra, he tore off a piece and offered it to her. Lysander could see how filthy his hands were, but with her hands tied behind her back, all Kassandra could do was nod. The Persian offered it to her lips and Kassandra took the food, chewing quickly. When she'd swallowed, Cleeto offered her another piece.

'Feed him,' said Kassandra, nodding to Lysander.

Cleeto obviously understood. He shifted until he was in front of Lysander, and held a piece of bread to his mouth. Lysander didn't want to take it, but he didn't know when he would next eat. He needed to keep his strength up. As he chewed, he saw Cleeto's eyes fall to his throat. Too late.

'No!' he began, but the Persian reached forward and tugged the Fire of Ares loose, snapping the thong around Lysander's neck. The red stone glinted in the late afternoon sun. Lysander fought against the ropes – they loosened a little, but not enough. All he could do was watch Cleeto tie the pendant around his own neck. He stuffed the remaining bread in Lysander's mouth and walked back to join his comrades.

'What's wrong?' said Kassandra.

Lysander spat the bread on to the deck.

'He's taken the Fire of Ares,' he said.

There was a shout from the bow of the ship. Vaumisa called out orders in Persian. His face was full of life. Lysander couldn't understand of course, but he heard one word repeated: 'Sarpedon'.

Was it true? Was his grandfather coming?

CHAPTER 23

Persians hurried across the deck, and lit torches along the edges. Through the dusk air Lysander could hear the unmistakable splash of oars in the water. There was a clunk, and a Persian lowered a ladder over the side of the ship. It creaked as someone put their weight on the rungs. A hand appeared on the rail.

Sarpedon climbed on to the deck. He was dressed simply, in a grey tunic and his red cloak. Dark shadows ringed his eyes, and the creases in his face seemed to have grown deeper, but he carried himself with dignity. His presence filled the deck. His eyes met Lysander's, and he gave a small bow of acknowledgment. Sarpedon turned and offered a hand to someone behind him. *Strabo!* Lysander realised.

'Welcome to my ship, Ephor,' said Vaumisa, waving a hand over the deck. 'We are honoured to have such a great warrior on board. We must dine together. It is not often I have the opportunity to meet as great a man as yourself.'

'And it is an honour to be here,' growled Sarpedon. 'Do you make a habit of tying up your guests? I trust children are no threat to a Persian general.'

Vaumisa nodded and Cleeto came towards Lysander and Kassandra with his knife. He sliced through their ropes, watching Lysander carefully.

Vaumisa led Sarpedon between the two columns of soldiers, to where a thick blanket and cushions had been laid on the deck. Lysander saw the Persians stand up straighter as the Spartan passed them, his back stiff and head held high. Vengeance burned in their eyes. Sarpedon sat opposite Vaumisa, who offered him a platter covered in meat, fruit and cheeses. As Sarpedon reached out, Lysander could see that his hand didn't tremble at all.

'Tell me, Sarpedon,' said the general, 'have you ever visited the Persian kingdom?'

'In my youth,' said Sarpedon, selecting a fig. 'It was an enjoyable excursion.'

'Oh yes?' said Vaumisa. 'How so?'

Sarpedon chewed slowly. 'I was fighting with the Lydians, south of Ephesus. I killed seventeen Persians in that campaign.' Vaumisa gave a tight smile. 'But I lost something too,' added Sarpedon, holding up the hand that was missing two fingers.

The general offered the platter again.

'Captivity does nothing for my appetite,' said Sarpedon, waving the food away.

'Some wine, then?' Vaumisa offered a two-handled

bowl to Sarpedon. 'I'm told it's the best in all of Greece, from the island of Thassos.'

Sarpedon drank deeply and wiped his lips.

'Did your pirates steal this too, Vaumisa?'

The general's face darkened, and all around the men's hands went to their short swords. Strabo closed his eyes and his lips moved in a silent prayer. *They're going to kill my grandfather!* thought Lysander. Vaumisa put up a hand.

'Spartans are not known for their hospitality,' said the Persian, 'so I will forgive your insults.'

'It is easy to forgive when you are hiding behind a man's grandchild, Vaumisa. Do not speak to me of hospitality.'

The general climbed to his feet, and Sarpedon did the same.

'I have great respect for you, Ephor. Your name is known across the seas in distant lands. You have fought many campaigns, bloody and long. It is a shame that such an illustrious career must come to an end.'

There was a movement above and Lysander saw a man standing on the mast, half concealed by the sail and holding a sword. He was staring down at Sarpedon, knees bent and ready to leap.

'Look out!' shouted Lysander. Sarpedon took a hasty step back and tripped on to the deck as the armed Persian leapt down. Lysander had to help his grandfather! He jumped to his feet and slammed into the Persian, sending the sword clattering on to the planks.

Weapons were drawn all around, and Vaumisa's body-guards quickly surrounded Sarpedon who was prone on the deck. The tips of their blades pointed at his chest.

Lysander grabbed the sword dropped by the assassin and charged at the Persians. He swiped aside two blades and lunged at a third man, but the three men came at him simultaneously. He had no chance. He ducked a stab to the head, but a kick landed in his stomach and doubled him over. The sword was knocked from his grasp, and strong hands pinned back his wrists and twisted his arms viciously behind him.

'Your troops in the north have been pushed back into the sea, Vaumisa,' Sarpedon growled. 'Your southern armies are vanquished also. You have lost. My death is no great victory.'

Kassandra threw herself at Vaumisa's feet.

'Please don't kill my grandfather!' she cried.

Vaumisa seized Kassandra's hair and pulled her up to standing, ignoring her screams. 'Cleeto, give word for the rowers to take their positions. We're going home.'

'Leave her,' Sarpedon bellowed across the deck. Lysander saw his grandfather try to stand, but the points of the swords pressed into his tunic, forcing him down. Blood stained his front.

Vaumisa shoved Kassandra towards Sarpedon. She fell across the deck and landed at her grandfather's feet. Lysander heard Cleeto shout below, and there was a splash of oars in the water. The ship lurched into motion.

'I've waited a long time for this day, Sarpedon,' said Vaumisa. 'And no grovelling child is going to take this moment from me. You dare to abuse my hospitality by boasting of your triumphs in my land. Well, you should know that one of those men you killed was my father.'

'If I killed your father, Vaumisa, he came looking for death.'

Vaumisa drew his sword and held the point at Sarpedon's throat. Lysander saw the twitch of a muscle in his grandfather's face, but otherwise he betrayed no emotion. Kassandra embraced Sarpedon, sobbing.

'You stabbed him through the belly with your sword, Spartan,' said Vaumisa. 'They brought him home, but it took him nine full days to die. Nine sleepless nights of agony.'

'He chose his path,' said Sarpedon. 'Such is a soldier's fate.'

'Fate!' bellowed Vaumisa. 'Yes, and your path will end on my sword.'

'You have me now,' said Sarpedon, pulling Kassandra close. 'Do as you will, but don't harm my grand-daughter. She has done nothing to provoke your anger.'

'Silence!' said Vaumisa. 'You, Spartan, do not give me orders. I will do whatever I wish.' He paced in front of Sarpedon. 'I can send messengers to all of the Greek world telling how you begged for your life, how you offered your granddaughter as a sacrifice for your own freedom. How you even offered to join forces with the

Persian empire against your own people.' Vaumisa was raging now. Spit dribbled down his chin and he stabbed a finger at Kassandra. 'I will cut out her tongue and say that you did it. The name of Sarpedon will be used whenever a Greek wants to call someone a coward.'

'You are a cruel man, Vaumisa,' said Sarpedon calmly. 'You would use my granddaughter to lure me on board. I pray the Gods send the Furies to torment every moment of your life.'

'The Gods!' scoffed Vaumisa. 'I *am* a God!' He nodded to his men. 'Hack off this Spartan's head and throw his body in the sea.'

'No!' screamed Kassandra.

Cleeto seized her shoulders and dragged her away. Lysander heaved against the hands that held him prisoner, but a kick to the back of his legs sent him to the deck. Two men seized Sarpedon, but he struggled against them. Another brought his sword hilt hard into Sarpedon's cheek. Lysander heard the bone crack, and his grandfather's knees gave way. Sobs racked Kassandra's body.

'Take him to the edge,' said Vaumisa. 'I don't want his Spartan blood on my deck.' The three Persians dragged Sarpedon to the rail at the edge of the deck.

'No!' said Lysander. He had to think fast. 'Kill me! I'm his grandson.'

Vaumisa spun around and lifted his hand. The executioners stayed their weapons.

'His grandson?' said Vaumisa. 'I thought Thorakis and

237

Demokrates were heirless but for this girl.'

'Don't listen to him . . .' slurred Sarpedon. He had been badly stunned by the strike of the sword hilt in his face.

'I was born out of marriage,' interrupted Lysander. 'After Thorakis was killed fighting the Tegeans.' Behind the ship, the shoreline of Greece was receding slowly. 'Why kill an old man? He's worthless now. He can barely hold a shield, and his spear thrust couldn't hurt a child.'

'I order you to silence!' shouted Sarpedon, his senses returning. But everyone could hear the desperation in his voice. Vaumisa gave a thin smile.

'If you take me,' urged Lysander, 'it will hurt Sarpedon far more, and it will rob Sparta of a warrior. Take me, a grandson for a father.' Lysander stepped up to Vaumisa, holding out his wrists, volunteering for capture. The Persians still held on to his upper arms.

Vaumisa nodded slowly. 'The son of Thorakis, here in my grasp. I'll send you, Sarpedon, back to Sparta with your pathetic granddaughter. She can nurse you in your old age. She can help you tend the graves of all your male descendants. You'll live in shame until the Gods decide to take pity and let you die.'

Lysander yanked himself free of his guards and went down on his knees in front of Vaumisa. He pulled his tunic aside, revealing his neck and chest.

'We can do it now,' he said. 'A sword through the throat.'

'Yes,' said Vaumisa. 'Let the Ephor see his grandson exhale his last breath. But no sword. We'll have a hanging. Let's see your body sway in the breeze, over Sarpedon's head.'

'No, no,' moaned Sarpedon. 'Lysander, what have you done?' Lysander felt a stab of guilt to see Sarpedon so distressed.

'Enough chatter,' said Vaumisa. 'Cleeto! Make a noose.'

The bodyguard picked up a section of rope and expertly tied it. Two others seized hold of Lysander.

'Grandfather,' whimpered Kassandra, tears streaming down her face. 'Do something . . .'

The rope was thrown over the boom – the horizontal spar along which the sail unfurled. The black eyes of the Persians burned into Lysander as he was jostled towards the waiting noose. He wasn't afraid. Not any more. The coarse rope was wrapped around his neck.

'It's the only way,' he told his grandfather.

Sarpedon's eyes were filled with tears and he let his gaze fall to the ship's floor.

'The old man can't bear to watch,' laughed Vaumisa. 'Make him!'

Two Persians sheathed their swords and seized Sarpedon by the shoulders. They twisted his head by the hair and neck so that he looked straight at Lysander.

'That's better,' said Vaumisa. 'Kill the boy, Cleeto.'

Lysander saw Cleeto tug on the rope. The rope grated on the jib above and the noose tightened around his neck. He heard Kassandra sobbing. First the soles of his feet left the planks, then the tips of his toes. The rope crushed his windpipe and fear overwhelmed him as his chest went tight and the blood pressure swelled in his head. His vision blurred.

'No!' yelled Sarpedon, grief tearing his voice. 'No! No! No!'

A hunched figure darted along the deck, brandishing a knife. Strabo!

'Persian scum!' shouted Sarpedon's slave. He lunged at Cleeto and the Persian, taken by surprise, let go of the rope. Lysander's feet slammed into the wooden planks, and he collapsed to his knees. He twisted round to see Cleeto swing his sword at Strabo. The slave lifted his arm to protect himself but the first blow sliced through his neck. He fell to the deck, writhing.

'Forgive me, master,' he said, before his eyes closed.

Violent coughing racked Lysander's body as he drew in air. *Strabo saved my life!* Vaumisa began desperately barking orders. Lysander saw Sarpedon punch his guard, who fell backwards into the water with a splash. Sarpedon swept down a hand and straightened up, lifting something that glittered in the air – he had a sword!

He swiped the blade before him, trying to keep the Persians at bay. But he was surrounded and Lysander realised with a thud of his heart that Sarpedon's sword

240

wasn't going to help him face off this number of enemies. *There's nowhere he can go*, thought Lysander. He tried to get to his feet to help, but his throat still scorched and dizziness made him fall back to his knees. As he watched helplessly, Sarpedon climbed backwards up the steps on to the forecastle. What was his grand-father doing?

'There's nowhere to escape to,' Vaumisa taunted.

Sarpedon lowered his sword and stared behind him, towards the shore of Spartan territory.

'Farewell, Lakedaimon,' he said. Lysander didn't understand.

Sarpedon turned around, and drew himself to his full height. He looked at Kassandra. Finally his eyes met Lysander's.

'Vaumisa,' he said. 'You wanted revenge. A life for a life?'

'And I will have it,' said the Persian. 'What choice do you have? You will see your grandson die.'

'There is always a choice,' said Sarpedon.

He took hold of the sword's hilt in both hands. Suddenly, Lysander knew what was coming.

'No!' he shouted. 'Don't do it!'

Sarpedon straightened his arms, bringing the tip of the sword to rest against his sternum. Kassandra cried out. 'Grandfather, please! No!'

Lysander rushed forward, pushing past the Persians.

'Here is your vengeance, Vaumisa!' Sarpedon shouted.

241

CHAPTER 24

Kassandra let out a wail and crumpled to the deck. Vaumisa cursed. A shudder racked Lysander's body as though a part of him had been ripped away.

Sarpedon froze, fixing Lysander with his gaze. Then he heaved the blade deeper still into his torso. Blood welled up and poured down Sarpedon's tunic and spattered on to the deck. His teeth were bared, like a wild animal. He staggered backwards and collapsed.

Lysander ran to his grandfather's side. A large pool of blood, darker than Sarpedon's cloak, spread out around him. Lysander threw himself down in the blood and pulled his grandfather's head on to his lap, and rested a hand on his chest. He could just feel the faint flutter of a heartbeat, slowing down.

'Why?' Lysander asked. Kassandra appeared beside him. Her tears mixed with the blood. She placed a small, delicate hand against her grandfather's cheek.

'How could you?' she cried. 'How could you leave us?'

Sarpedon placed a hand on top of Lysander's. His cheek was bruised from where he'd been struck with the sword hilt, and his face was deathly pale, but he managed a thin smile.

'Yours was not the sacrifice the Gods demanded,' Sarpedon gasped. 'Tell the Council I died like a true Spartan.'

'I will,' said Lysander. Sarpedon's grip softened and he closed his eyes.

A shadow fell over them – Vaumisa. He gazed down at Sarpedon's body. Then something else caught Vaumisa's attention. He looked up.

Lysander followed his line of vision. Around the tip of the peninsula, the prow of a ship cut through the water. It surged through the waves, powered by a triple tier of oars. Another ship followed in its wake. Then another. *A rescue party!*

'Spartans!' said Vaumisa loudly. He turned and climbed to the deck, barking orders in his native tongue.

The Persians scrambled across the deck, seizing bows and quivers. Vaumisa bellowed furiously, and pointed to where Lysander and Kassandra were standing beside Sarpedon's body. The archers turned and hurried to string their arrows.

'We have to jump!' shouted Lysander, grabbing Kassandra's arm.

She pulled back. 'I can't leave my grandfather!'

There was no time to argue. Lysander slipped his

arm around her waist and propelled her towards the edge of the platform. Her legs wheeled as she fell through the air towards the water. Lysander launched off behind her, hearing the soft *pffft* of an arrow pass his ear.

The water took him. Kassandra was already at the surface and he swam up beside her. She was panting with panic and cold. The Persians were lining the deck above, aiming their bows.

'Back down!' he shouted, pushing her head beneath the water.

Arrows darted silently through the water around them, trailing white bubbles. He grabbed Kassandra's hand and kicked hard. She seemed to understand and pulled her hand free, swimming beside him under-water. Lysander swam until his lungs were close to bursting, then broke the surface with Kassandra beside him.

'Are you hurt?' he shouted to Kassandra.

'No,' she gasped. 'I don't think so.'

The Persian ship was about twenty paces away. They were firing arrows at the approaching Greek ships now. As the trireme drew closer, Lysander could see the soldiers lined up along the decks, spears at the ready. Every time a volley of arrows arced above them, they took shelter beneath their shields in unison. The oars lifted chaotically in the Persian ship and began to churn the water. They were trying to escape.

'Help!' shouted Kassandra. 'Over here!'

Lysander joined his voice with hers, until a soldier on the nearest Greek ship spotted them and shouted an order back to his helmsman.

The ship split from the others and came towards them. As it drifted alongside, a ladder was thrown over. Lysander held Kassandra by the waist and thrust her out of the water. A soldier reached from above and pulled her up. Lysander followed, shivering as he climbed the ladder. He only just had the strength to hang on. Two hands gripped him under the armpits and lifted him the rest of the way.

He was standing face-to-face with Demaratos.

'Sarpedon?' he asked urgently. 'Is he safe?'

Lysander shook his head. Demaratos placed a hand on his shoulder.

'I'm sorry. He was a great warrior. We will avenge his death. Come on,' he said. 'There are Persians to capture.'

A Spartan soldier had thrown his cloak around Kassandra's shoulders. She came to Lysander's side, shivering with cold, her sodden hair sticking to her face. He put his arm around her and the two of them gazed out to sea.

Lysander's ship was last in the pursuit now, and the others were close behind Vaumisa's fleeing ship. Lysander could see Vaumisa standing on the forecastle of the Persian ship, anxiously looking back and shouting orders to his men. But they were tiring. The oars didn't move with such speed any longer. The first two Greek ships were level now, one on each side, about two boat-lengths away. Lust for vengeance boiled in the pit of Lysander's stomach. His grandfather's death would not be for nothing.

'Row faster!' shouted the commander on Lysander's ship.

As the first Greek ship closed in, Lysander could see Vaumisa abandon his platform.

'That's right,' said Demaratos from Lysander's side. 'Run away if you can.'

The reinforced prow of the Greek ship crashed into the stern of Vaumisa's vessel, shattering the hull and sending splinters of wood flying through the air. The oars on the port side of the boat jammed in the water, and it came to a sudden halt, turning jarringly in the water. The second Greek ship came from the other side, and rammed home into the starboard. In the chaos, Lysander saw the Persian hull splinter. As the planks crumbled into the water, he stared into the belly of the ship. Water gushed in and screams of panic filled the air.

'Take these,' said Demaratos, handing Lysander a shield and spear. 'Kassandra – go below. It's not safe here.'

'I'm not afraid,' she said coldly. 'I want to see Vaumisa brought to justice.'

Their vessel was drawing alongside now, and adrenalin surged through every one of Lysander's limbs. The Persian deck was in chaos, as oarsmen and soldiers armed themselves for combat. Lysander could no longer see Vaumisa.

'Reel them in!' ordered the commander. Soldiers standing on the edge of the boat swung ropes armed with hooks on to the Persian ship. The irons bit home, and immediately the Spartans began pulling the Persian ship towards their own. The water churned with foam beneath the ships and Lysander watched as Persians who'd fallen into the water were crushed as the two hulls ground together. The Spartans gave a blood-curdling cry and poured on to the Persian deck, spears held high. Lysander jumped as well, followed by Demaratos. Lysander thrust his spear at the nearest Persian. The tip ripped across his belly and spilled his guts over the deck. Lysander turned the spear around and smashed the lizard-sticker into the prone soldier's cheek, killing him instantly.

The Persians were outnumbered. Some were already giving up, but the Spartans showed them no mercy other than a quick death. But where was Vaumisa? Lysander scoured the deck, threading through the slaughter. He climbed on to the platform and saw Sarpedon's body lying where they had left it. His peaceful face showed nothing of the trauma he had undergone. If it wasn't for the sword's hilt sticking out of his chest, and the pool of thick black blood, he might have died in his sleep. Lysander fought back his tears. The rear end of the ship listed as water flooded the hull, and Lysander stumbled to keep his balance.

The vessel wouldn't be afloat for much longer.

Then Lysander saw Vaumisa.

In the dark water, forty paces further out, the Persian general was making away in Sarpedon's rowing boat, with Cleeto heaving desperately at the oars.

Lysander shouldered his spear.

'Persian!' he shouted. Vaumisa sat in the small boat and stared back. Lysander couldn't make out his expression. It didn't matter to him now.

Lysander pulled back his spear arm. He focused along the shaft, as his tutor had taught him. 'Never throw your spear unless you really have to,' Diokles had always said.

I have to, whispered Lysander to himself.

He launched the spear, following through with the throwing arm for maximum power.

Vaumisa had nowhere to run.

The tip caught him beneath the neck and burst through the other side, showering Cleeto with gore. The general's hands went to his throat as the blood sprayed over his torso and into the water around. His eyes went wide with shock, and Lysander heard a guttural noise as Vaumisa began to choke on his own blood. The Persian toppled forward, his face smashing into the edge of the rowing boat with the full force of his body's bulk. The boat rocked perilously. Vaumisa's hands scrabbled at his throat as he writhed like a fish suffocating in the air. Cleeto cowered at the back of the boat. Vaumisa jerked suddenly and slammed sideways. A wave of water swamped the vessel and Cleeto tried desperately to keep the boat steady by throwing himself to the opposite side. It wasn't enough. It tipped over, sending both men into the dark water.

Cleeto's head broke the surface, and his hands thrashed. All Lysander heard was a muffled cry. Then he was gone. Lysander watched the surface for any other signs of life. There were none. Vaumisa was dead.

May the Furies torment you for eternity, Lysander prayed. Then he turned away.

CHAPTER 25

The damaged Persian ship lurched, and the bow lifted out of the water.

'It's sinking!' shouted Demaratos. The other Spartans were already jumping back on to their own ship. Lysander looked at his grandfather's body.

'I can't go without Sarpedon,' said Lysander. 'Help me with him.'

Demaratos nodded, and came to the base of the platform. Lysander pulled the sword from Sarpedon's body, and placed the weapon in his own sheath. A small well of blood escaped the fatal wound. He placed two hands under Sarpedon's mighty shoulders. The body was still warm, and it crushed Lysander's heart to think of the life that had seeped away. He managed to move his grandfather's corpse to the edge of the platform where Demaratos could reach the legs.

'Ready?' Lysander asked Demaratos. His friend gave a single nod as he prepared to take the weight. Lysander cradled his grandfather's head gently while

Demaratos held his legs. Between them, they lowered the corpse. The timbers of the Persian ship creaked.

The Spartans were already uncoupling their hooks from the ship, preparing to depart.

'Help us!' shouted Lysander. 'This man is an Ephor of Sparta.'

A small group came over to assist Lysander and Demaratos. When Demaratos and the body were safely aboard the Spartan ship, Lysander clambered over as well.

Lysander and his friend stood side by side, watching in silence as the Persian vessel was swallowed by the waves. Soon all that remained were corpses, floating in the sea water amongst the debris of weapons and timber.

The waves slapped against the hull of the ship as it came to a halt at the jetty at Gytheion. The shoreline was crowded with soldiers, bloodied and filthy from battle. Most of the small buildings and fishing boats were no more than blackened, charred remains. The Ephor called Myron stood on the landing gangway below, with a dozen Spartan soldiers standing in his wake.

'Where is Vaumisa?' he called up.

'He's dead,' said Demaratos. 'Lysander killed him.'

The Ephor looked hard at Lysander.

'Sparta thanks you, son of Thorakis. You have proved yourself a brave warrior. And Sarpedon?'

Demaratos was silent, and Lysander could not bring himself to speak.

'Come, where is the Ephor?' said Myron.

Lysander fought to control his voice. 'He's . . . dead.' Myron's face took on a sheen of disbelief as he heard the news. 'He sacrificed his own life,' continued Lysander, 'so that Kassandra and I could live.'

Myron was silent, but the soldiers behind him exchanged glances and murmurs. One whispered, 'It cannot be true.'

'And his body?' said Myron eventually.

'We rescued it,' said Lysander, gesturing behind him. Sarpedon's body was lying on a makeshift stretcher of sailcloth and ship's planks. Kassandra, her face deathly pale, sat at his side, holding the old man's hand. Myron climbed the bow ladder, and pulled himself up to the handrail to look on to the deck. The truth confirmed, he sank back to the jetty.

The Ephor nodded slowly, his jaw set firm and his eyes far away. 'The Council must be told,' he muttered. Then he turned back to Lysander. 'Sarpedon is lucky to have you as a descendant.' The tears itched behind Lysander's eyes – he blinked them away. 'He must be taken to Sparta immediately, and given a hero's funeral.' He turned to his men. 'Arrange a cart. I want one of you to ride ahead. Take the fastest horse, and tell them to inform the Elders that Sarpedon is dead.'

'I'll escort the body,' said Lysander. He couldn't bear the thought of leaving his grandfather's side.

'Very well,' said Myron. 'Bring horses for these Spartans,' he ordered.

Lysander turned and looked back to Kassandra. Demaratos crouched beside her and she was trembling with the cold. He realised that he was her only real family now.

He hobbled back towards them. Every step sent pain through his injured calf, but the wound was already scabbed with blood, and there was no sign of infection.

'We have to go,' he said.

Kassandra looked up at him, her eyes hollow with grief. Demaratos lifted her hand from Sarpedon's and helped her to her feet.

While they watched, Sarpedon's body was transferred from the ship to a waiting cart. Two horses were harnessed into place, and a Spartan soldier came out from amongst the crowd. Lysander didn't recognise him, with all the dirt and blood that crusted his face.

'Greetings, friend.' The voice told him who it was.

'Greetings, Leonidas,' replied Lysander.

Leonidas threw his arms around Lysander's shoulders and held him in an embrace. Behind him, Lysander spotted Orpheus, resting against an upturned rowing boat. A surgeon had obviously seen to him. There was nothing below his knee, and a bandage heavy with blood covered the stump. He was pale, but he managed to raise a hand in Lysander's direction.

'Lysander,' said Myron. He turned to the Ephor, who was holding the reins of a horse. Lysander recognised that it was Pegasus, Sarpedon's finest stallion. 'Ride to Sparta with Sarpedon.'

'Thank you,' said Lysander, stroking Pegasus' flank. Demaratos helped Kassandra into the back of the cart and jumped in beside her. Myron came forward with a fleece and handed it to Demaratos. He draped it around Kassandra's shoulders.

Suddenly shouts stirred from further along the shore. Two Spartan soldiers were dragging a figure between them and he shouted curses in his own tongue.

As they reached Myron and Lysander, they threw him to the ground.

'Cleeto!' Lysander exclaimed.

'Sir,' one of the Spartans addressed the Ephor. 'We found this Persian trying to climb ashore at the rocks.'

'Do you know this villain, Lysander?'

Lysander nodded. 'Yes, he tried to hang me on board Vaumisa's vessel. He was one of the general's personal guards.'

Myron looked at Cleeto in disgust.

'Then his life is yours, Lysander. What would you have us do with him?'

Lysander looked at where Vaumisa's henchman knelt, still dripping saltwater. He remembered how he had knotted the noose and placed it over his neck. How he had pulled on the rope that almost killed him.

Lysander drew Sarpedon's sword. Cleeto stiffened when he saw the blade. Lysander flexed his fingers around the handle and stepped slowly towards Cleeto.

After a day on the battlefield, he knew how easy it was to take another man's life. Cleeto bowed his head, exposing the back of his neck. Lysander placed the tip of the sword against the ridges of the Persian's spine, where head met torso. One thrust would do it.

Lysander adjusted his hands on the hilt, but instead of ramming the blade home, he twisted it under the leather thong that encircled the Persian's neck. The Fire of Ares clattered on to the ground. Lysander stooped and retrieved it, stroking the familiar jewel with the pad of his thumb.

He walked over to Myron, leaving Cleeto on his knees.

'I have seen enough death today,' he said, sheathing the sword. Lysander tied the Fire of Ares back where it belonged – around his own neck. He made his way towards Pegasus.

'What shall we do with the prisoner?' asked Myron.

Lysander turned and looked at Cleeto, cowering beside the Ephor.

'Send him back to Persia to tell of our victory,' said Lysander.

Placing his foot in the stirrup, he climbed into the saddle.

'Thorakis would be proud of you,' said the Ephor, before slapping the carthorses into motion. As the cart moved away from the shore, Lysander felt his father's spirit closer than ever.

★   ★   ★

Demaratos comforted Kassandra as they passed the battlefields where the Spartans and Persians had fought. Lysander rode in silence through the devastation. The ground was littered with bodies – Spartans and Persians together. In places, the ground was soaked red with blood. So many had died. Hilarion, Ariston, Diokles. So many others whose names he'd never know. How many empty beds would there be in the dormitory now?

It was almost dawn when they reached the outskirts of Sparta. Looking back, Lysander saw that Kassandra's eyes were closed in sleep and she leant heavily against Demaratos's chest.

The first person they met was a young Helot woman, cradling a baby at her breast. She held out a pink flower as they passed, and Lysander leant from the saddle to take it.

'Thank you,' he said. Her silent gesture lifted Lysander's spirits. Without the Spartan sacrifice, who knew what the Persians would have done to the Helot population?

As they made their way into the streets of Sparta, men and women, Helots and free-dwellers, came out of their houses. They shouted words of triumph and encouragement as Lysander led the cart past.

'Bless you!' said an old man, turning to an elderly woman by his side. 'We're saved, Nylix. We're saved!'

'Praise the Gods,' she said. 'Praise Sparta!'

As Lysander came nearer to the agora – the market-place at the foot of the acropolis – he caught sight of

Spartan soldiers ahead. They lined the road on one side, standing straight-backed and staring ahead, their spears vertical. The sight swelled Lysander with pride.

He reached the first in the line, and the Spartan pushed out his spear arm, holding the shaft steady. His neighbour did the same. And the next man, and the next. *They're saluting me!* Lysander drew Sarpedon's sword from its sheath, and held it out to each, tapping the tips of their spears with the end of his blade.

At one end of the agora stood the round Council House. The marketplace was almost empty of people. Torches rested in tall iron tripods at regular intervals around the outside. Spartan soldiers stood between them in rows, four men deep. In the centre three carts had gathered. Each carried long planks of wood. Between them, a structure was being built by a team of carpenters. Lysander immediately recognised what it was. A funeral pyre. He dismounted from his horse, and the cart with Sarpedon's body stopped behind him.

One of the Spartan soldiers at the edge of the marketplace lifted a horn to his lips and gave a long blast. Moments later, the heavy bronze door of the Council House creaked open, and from inside stepped a Spartan whom Lysander hadn't seen before. He was of medium height, with a narrow, gnarled face and blue eyes. Behind him came the Ephor Tellios and then the rest of the Elders. They proceeded slowly across the agora until they reached Lysander.

'Greetings, son of Thorakis,' said the leader. 'I am

Cleomenes, one of the two Kings of Sparta.'

Lysander climbed out of the saddle and dropped to his knees, his head reeling. *A King!*

'Forgive me, Your Majesty.'

King Cleomenes placed a hand on Lysander's head, signalling him to rise.

'There is no need to kneel, my boy. A King in Sparta is the same as any other man: a soldier.'

Lysander stood up and looked the King in the eye.

'Sarpedon . . . he's . . .'

'The Council has been told,' said Cleomenes. 'Have no fear. He will be given a funeral like a hero of old. But first, let our wives, good women of Sparta all, prepare the body. You must cleanse yourself in the river, also.' He turned to the soldier who had blown the horn. 'Chrysippus, find Lysander clean garments.'

Lysander followed the King's orders, washing the blood and dirt from his body in the river Eurotas, and dressing himself in a clean tunic, sandals and cloak. When he returned to the agora he felt as though he had been born anew. The soldiers from outside the marketplace had moved in around the funeral pyre. Behind them stood crowds of free-dwellers and Helots, the crowds stretching back into the surrounding streets. As Lysander approached, the people parted to let him pass, calling out thanks, or simply bowing their heads.

At the edge of the agora, a Spartan came forward, and handed a torch to Lysander. 'You must light the pyre, son of Thorakis, to speed the great Sarpedon to the fields of Elysion, where the shades of heroes walk in the Underworld.'

Lysander took the flaming bundle of sticks, and walked solemnly back to the centre of the agora. His breath misted the air, but he didn't feel the cold. He felt a new flame burning within him.

He climbed the wooden steps up to the edge of the pyre, and stood still, taking in Sarpedon's corpse for the last time. Dressed in a clean white tunic, his arms were folded over his chest, his hands wrapped around the hilt of his sword, which lay flat along his front. He was wearing his red cloak. The women had trimmed his beard and combed back his hair, and although he wasn't diminished in death, there was no doubt in Lysander's mind that his grandfather's spirit had left him. *Are you walking the fields of Elysion?* he whispered. *Are you walking with Thorakis, your son?*

Lysander looked down into the marketplace. King Cleomenes and the Elders were all watching him, and as he looked at each of them in turn, they gave a bow of respect. Then they parted and Kassandra came forward. She was standing straight, dressed in a clean white dress, with her hair tied up and her head high. Her eyes were dry of tears. Demaratos came behind her, and placed a comforting hand on her shoulder.

'Behold Spartans!' Lysander shouted, holding the torch aloft. 'Behold free-dwellers and Helots! Here lies the Ephor Sarpedon! He died as he lived, with courage, with honour.' Lysander paused to let his words sink in. 'Today we have earned victory over the Persians, but be in no doubt, the price has been heavy. Sparta has lost the best of men!' He thought of Ariston, of Hilarion, of Diokles. He thought of Thyestes and his courage as he awaited death.

Lysander lowered the torch to the dry kindling near Sarpedon's bare feet. The twigs caught with a crackle. He moved the torch along the length of the pyre, making sure the funeral bier would burn evenly. As the smoke rose to his eyes and Sarpedon's cloak began to blacken at the edges, he climbed down.

Spartan soldiers crowded around him at the base of the pyre and one took the torch from him. Before he could do anything else, two others had hoisted him on to their shoulders. One of them shouted, 'Lysander!' at the top of his lungs. 'Lysander!' said two more behind him.

Others joined in, until all the Spartans were shouting his name. Then the Helots and free-dwellers took up the chant as well.

'Lysander! Lysander! Lysander!'

He was carried aloft through the agora, and saw Demaratos and Kassandra behind. The faces of the crowd, rapt with joy, were lifted to his, and their arms reached into the air as they called out his name.

Lysander looked over the heads of the crowd. The heat of Sarpedon's pyre reminded him how much he had lost, how much had been given for this victory. His father, mother and now his grandfather were all gone. He was almost alone in the world. But maybe not. All of the men and women that surrounded him were his people: not only the Spartans, but the free-dwellers and Helots who lived in the same land. For this, Lysander had fought. And for this, Lysander would fight another day.